"What Did You Do To My Fiancé?"

Cathy asked Rafe.

"He's okay. Let's get back to the important stuff—us."

She glared at him.

"He's taking a little nap in his closet."

"Rafe!"

"I'm afraid I handcuffed him and tied and gagged him."

"Dear God!" Forgetting she didn't have a stitch on, Cathy threw back the sheet. "I've got to let him out."

For one long moment, Rafe stared down at her, hypnotized, the mere sight of her naked body making desire flood through him. Hungrily his eyes slid over her. If he let her go now, he would lose her forever.

"Not till I prove to you that you love me," Rafe murmured, pulling her back into his arms.

Dear Reader,

This month it seems like everyone's in romantic trouble.
We have runaway brides and jilted grooms....They've
been left at the altar and wonder if they'll *ever* find true
love with the right person.

Of course they do, and we get to find out how, as we
read Silhouette Desire's delightful month of "Jilted!"
heroes and heroines.

And what better way to start this special month
than with *The Accidental Bridegroom*, a second
1994 *Man of the Month* from one of your favorites,
Ann Major? I'm sure you'll enjoy this passionate story
of seduction and supposed betrayal as much as I do.

And look for five more fabulous books by some of your
most beloved writers: Dixie Browning, Cait London,
Raye Morgan, Jennifer Greene and Cathie Linz. Yes,
their characters might have been left at the altar...but
they don't stay single for long!

So don't pick and choose—read about them all! I loved
these stories, and I'm sure you will, too.

Lucia Macro
Senior Editor

Please address questions and book requests to:
Silhouette Reader Service
U.S.: 3010 Walden Ave., P.O. Box 1325, Buffalo, NY 14269
Canadian: P.O. Box 609, Fort Erie, Ont. L2A 5X3

ANN MAJOR
THE ACCIDENTAL BRIDEGROOM

SILHOUETTE *Desire®*

Published by Silhouette Books

America's Publisher of Contemporary Romance

SILHOUETTE BOOKS

ISBN 0-373-05889-6

THE ACCIDENTAL BRIDEGROOM

Books by Ann Major

ANN MAJOR

is not only a successful author, but she also manages a business and runs a busy household with three children. She lists traveling and playing the piano among her many interests. Her favorite composer, quite naturally, is the romantic Chopin.

I owe a special thank-you to several people:

To Tara Gavin for asking me to write this book and
encouraging me during the months when I had
writer's block.

To Ron Coetzee, a private investigator and a real-life
hero—for sharing some of his insights into his
fascinating and dangerous profession. It was Ron who
gave me the "spark" for my hero and this book.

To Patricia Patterson for introducing me to Ron and for
all the secretarial and research assistance she
constantly does.

To my cousin, Diane Donaho, for helping with some of
my initial research and for proofing my rusty Spanish.

To my daughter, Kimberly Cleaves, for gathering
research on Mexico's Day of the Dead in her
high school library.

To Ted for his support and love and for listening
to me whine.

I know this is a short book, and I am thanking a lot of
people. But I had a lot of trouble writing this book, and
I feel very grateful to everyone who helped me.

Prologue

Rock and roll music drifted out of the mock French château behind the high white wall. The rich brats at the Calderon party sounded like they were having a hell of a good time, and maybe they were. Frankly, Rafe Steele felt too sulky and bored to give a damn. His pain pill had worn off, and the nine stitches in the middle of his back where a green-haired woman had bitten him last night had begun to throb.

It was Saturday night, his first night back in his hometown, Houston. He was dead tired from a six-month marathon in L.A. guarding JoJo and his heavy-metal band of crazies. Rafe needed to relax and that meant doing something interesting that would take his mind off things. He would have preferred a hot date or some kind of action, or even his TV remote and a good bottle of booze.

Anything would have been better than hanging out here. It wasn't that River Oaks Boulevard with its fancy big houses and sweeping lawns and shady live oaks was too rich for his blood. It was that it was too damned dull.

At least that's what he told himself.

Maybe a lot of poor suckers thought this was the lifestyle to die for. Maybe they got their kicks out of mile-long reflecting pools and yards full of naked statues and dozens of pretentious fountains. Rafe had seen the spread on this place in the *Houston Post*. That's how he knew the inside was even gaudier. There were twenty-one-foot ceilings, tall windows and eleven-foot arched doorways. The swirling black-marble stairway was the talk of the town. Everything in these houses was meant to impress. And everyone, too.

Who needed it?

Rafe had read somewhere that the rich were different.

Nobody had to tell him that. Not when his own father—

Rafe decided not to get going on that one.

Yeah, the rich were meaner and greedier and phonier. They had to have *more;* they wanted people to think they were better and smarter. But the downside was they had way more to hide.

So—who needed them? Any of them? Especially a slimeball like Calderon.

You, you dumb jerk. You make your living protecting them. Down deep you think they are better and smarter.

Unbidden came the memory of a blue-eyed little boy standing on the wrong side of another wall, wanting to be acknowledged by the man on the other side more than anything.

Rafe struck a match, hunkering low and cupping his hands to hide the glare that lit his lean, harsh features, which were sullenly handsome in that dangerous way most women found so attractive. He inhaled deeply, and lazily watched the azure smoke of his cigarette drift up through the warm night air.

There were at least a dozen off-duty cops guarding every entrance and every exit.

So what the hell was he doing here, skulking around in the shadows like some spy on a cloak-and-dagger mission? Rafe could've strangled Manuel for giving Armi Calderon the glowing recommendation that had landed him this baby-sitting job guarding Armi's twenty-year-old stepdaughter, Cathy, who was home from college. Because Calderon had *had* to have him then.

Manuel, Rafe's boss, had been right in the middle of giving Rafe a rash of heat for walking out on JoJo Johnson when the phone had rung. They'd been shoving a bottle of booze back and forth across Manuel's desk, discussing the matter like any two normal professionals... at the top of their lungs.

Manuel had been yelling that even the JoJos of the world deserved the best protection money could buy, that that's what his security agency was all about, that that's why guys like Rafe who couldn't fit in anywhere else had jobs.

Rafe had been defending himself, defying Manuel to find anyone stupid enough to stick with JoJo day and night for more than six months—especially after one of JoJo's cuties had bitten a hunk out of his back when he'd told her JoJo already had company and had escorted her out of the star's suite.

When Rafe had yanked up his black T-shirt so Manuel could see the big white bandage in the center of his lean, hard-muscled back, Manuel had studied the dragon tattoo on Rafe's left biceps, instead. "Where the hell did you get that?"

"Singapore. The navy. Back when I was a sucker for Chinese art," Rafe drawled lazily.

"Then you should love JoJo. JoJo's an artist. He's the world's biggest—"

Manuel was about to say *rock star* but Rafe beat him to the punch with a string of descriptive curse words. Rafe was just warming up when Calderon's call had come in.

"Armi—" Manuel had broken off in a hush, his face grim as he motioned Rafe to shut up, whispering hoarsely, "This may be your big chance to redeem your-self, Steele."

"Oh, no, you don't! I want the week off."

Manuel had flipped on the speaker so Rafe could hear, too.

"I want an extra bodyguard—tonight," Calderon's voice boomed. "Chris is throwing Cathy a big party, and there's been another death threat, amigo. I need a new man for a few days, somebody nobody around here knows. Someone just for Cathy."

"No problem, Armi."

"You don't understand." The brash voice lost its bluster. "Cathy *is* a problem. She's run off everybody my regular security people have put on the job. I need some-one very experienced with uncooperative clients. That's why I thought of your operation."

"Well..." Dubiously, Manuel studied Rafe's un-shaven face, his long black ponytail and his single, glit-tering earring.

"You told me you didn't want me protecting women anymore," Rafe mouthed silently.

Manuel frowned as if he was remembering Consuelo, too. "Well, some of my guys are a little too...er...rough-cut for someone as carefully protected as your daughter."

"You owe me, amigo, big time."

A shadow passed over Manuel's face. "Right," he said. "I'll find someone. But on such short notice, it's going to cost you."

"Fine. Cathy won't stand for another uptight jerk with a crew cut bossing her around."

It was then that a slow grin had spread across Manuel's heavy features and he'd reached across his desk and yanked Rafe's shoulder-length ponytail meaningfully. "No crew cut, amigo."

Rafe erupted out of his seat like a cannonball. Booze shot everywhere. "Oh, no, you don't, amigo!"

"You should have cut your hair when I told you to," Manuel whispered, chuckling as he mopped his perspiring forehead.

"What was that?" Armi demanded.

"Just one of my...er...rough-cut guys."

"And she can't even suspect this guy's a bodyguard."

"Believe me—she won't."

"Damn it, I said no!" Rafe thundered, grabbing his leather biker's jacket with all the flashy zippers and storming to the door, zippers jangling as loudly as his nerves.

"Steele, you walk out on this one, and you're fired!" Returning to Calderon, Manuel said smoothly, "Sorry... How does long hair, a dragon tattoo and an earring sound? I have a guy who's been protecting a heavy-metal rock star and his group. He's a little rough around the edges, but he ought to be able to handle one well-bred young lady."

"He's perfect."

"Perfect..." Manuel's keen dark gaze flickered over Rafe. "Maybe. Let's keep our fingers crossed she goes for his pretty blue eyes."

End of conversation. End of the pleasant week off Rafe had planned. But the beginning of his burning determination to go into business for himself with Mike.

Before Rafe had stormed out, Manuel warned softly, "Watch yourself. Calderon is dangerous. We go back a long way—to Mexico. He's a hell of a lot tougher and a hell of a lot meaner and way way smarter than that singing piece of scum JoJo Johnson. Don't get creative. Just take care of his daughter. He won't understand a stunt like you pulled with my daughter."

"No handcuffs, I promise," Rafe said. "And—just for the record—I never laid a hand on your precious Consuelo... even though she tried to get very friendly."

"You wouldn't be alive if she hadn't convinced me of the same thing."

"*She's* alive because of what I did."

"Which is why I give you so many career-advancement opportunities, amigo. Like tonight."

"Yeah. Right."

Rafe blew a smoke ring and peered through it at the high white wall. So far, he hadn't seen hide nor hair of his precious charge. But he knew what she looked like. She was just another typical rich girl—tall and skinny with a lot of golden hair. She'd probably grow up to be another boring socialite like her much-written-about mother.

So here he was, watching the princess's heavily guarded castle wall and waiting, the growing mountain of cigarette butts by his right boot proof he'd been there for hours.

He inhaled again and blew a couple of smoke rings; hell, there was nothing better to do.

And then—

He saw it.

Over where the oak tree grew by the wall.

At first he thought it was just a bit of moonlight glittering on the top of the wall. Even so, he felt a rush as he squashed out his cigarette and lifted his binoculars.

Like shooting stars, a pair of sequined high heels sailed over the wall.

Next came a slim naked foot with scarlet-tipped toes. Rafe couldn't see the rest of the girl because she was behind the tree.

He focused on the long, skinny foot. He'd guess size ten, but even so, somehow it was dainty.

There was no way to know if the foot belonged to Cathy, but Rafe didn't care much after he saw the leg. It was shapely and gorgeous; it got him hot instantly. So hot he had to remind himself that he was on a job and that he was a professional.

Then he saw the rest of her as she eased her body down the trunk onto the wall. Her fluid grace made him remember the way a particularly talented topless dancer had slithered up and down a pole in a dive he'd visited when he'd last done undercover.

Not that this girl was topless, but the low-cut white chiffon dress that rode up her slim, voluptuous curves left too little to a male imagination as expert and fertile as Rafe's. She was too tall—and too skinny for his usual taste, but tonight he didn't much care. She had a shock of fiery gold hair that spilled out of two diamond clips. A single strand of diamonds sparkled at her throat. Her high cheekbones gave her slender face a natural elegance, and she had the sweetest, most kissable, generous mouth.

He sucked in a sharp breath as he recognized the Calderon girl. In no way had the photograph captured her potential. She radiated vitality that made him know she would sizzle like a live wire.

She leaned down to help someone on the other side of the wall. Then a man in a tux swung a wobbly leg up beside her and straddled the wall. He teetered from side to side, and she tried to steady him. But he fell to the sidewalk, anyway, collapsing in a heap in the azaleas.

As lithely as a cat, Cathy jumped down beside him. But when she had him untangled from the hedge, he grabbed her and began to kiss and paw her. She struggled loose and ran down the street away from the house, fumbling with her purse. But he ran after her, staggering clumsily as he seized her by the waist and hurled her against the wall. Ruthlessly he pulled her against him and turned her face to his, devouring her mouth. She kicked and lashed out, but the brute was so liquored-up he just laughed as he dragged her to the ground. The diamond necklace was ripped from her throat.

Rafe had seen enough. In seconds, his long legs were loping across the street. Then his fingers were digging into the surprisingly hard muscles of the big lout's neck and yanking him off. But as Rafe did so, the girl got in the way. When Rafe stomped down on those scarlet-tipped, bare toes, she screamed and kicked him, throwing him off-balance. He had to glance down to make sure he wouldn't hurt her again. The drunk spun around, and cracked a fist through Rafe's jaw.

As the world blackened, the girl jerked a can out of her purse and squirted wildly. Too wildly, because Rafe's eyes and nose and mouth smarted as if she'd sprayed him with acid.

He couldn't see. He couldn't breathe. His nose was running; his sinuses burned all the way back to his brain.

Then the other guy hit him again, and Rafe careened backward. His head hit concrete, and he went out like a bad light bulb.

When Rafe came to a minute or so later, his burning head was nestled in a soft, white chiffon lap. Delicate, light fingers were stroking the whiskers of his unshaven cheek. Those same fingers moved to his earring and lifted his ponytail.

Through slitted black lashes he peered warily at the girl's anxious face.

"I'm sorry," she whispered contritely. "My aim was off."

Her lush breasts crushed his forehead when she bent closer. Her hair fell out of her clips and about her cheeks in sexy tangles. He caught the scent of lavender soap.

Unconventional bodyguard meets difficult client. In spite of his burning sinuses and his anger that she probably thought him an incompetent wimp, he decided maybe this wasn't so bad, after all.

Rafe groaned, and she jumped. His hand went to the bump at the back of his head. There was an acidic, peppery taste in his mouth, and his nasal passages stung every time he rasped for air.

But she smelled so good in spite of his injured sinuses, and his view of those luscious globes was so fantastic, he began to care less about the rest.

Watch yourself, Steele. "Where's the guy who slugged me?" he demanded.

"Jeff?" She beamed proudly. "I got rid of him—"

Major male-ego attack. *Major.* He was supposed to be protecting her. *"You—"*

Saucily she shook a little white spray can. "It's something I ordered out of one of my bodyguard's catalogs."

Rafe sat up slowly, rubbing his head. Little stars were whirling round and round. Vengefully, he ripped the white can out of her hand and tossed it into the gutter.

"Hey—you!"

When she made like she was going to jump up and get it, he grabbed her slender wrist in a viselike grip.

"Hey—*you!* That stuff is dangerous—in the hands of a maniac!" His hard blue eyes fastened on her startled face. "Or a nitwit! You're supposed to spray the bad guy, not the good guy."

"So—which one are you?"

"You've got a smart mouth, Skinny. *I* didn't try to jump you in the bushes." He stood all the way up, but as he dusted himself off, she got up too and gave him the once-over again. Her sharp dark gaze got him hot as it climbed slowly up his black cowboy boots and black, denim-clad thighs to his leather jacket.

She yanked at the zipper of his biker jacket. Then she flipped the tip of his glossy ponytail. "How am I supposed to tell you're the good guy if you dress like a cheap biker thug?"

He brushed at the dirt on the leather garment in question. "Hey, this jacket wasn't cheap."

"Then you got ripped off, hon."

The way *hon* slid through her pretty, scarlet-tinted lips so softly turned him on more. Which was dangerous.

"You should take a lady with you when you go shopping," she said.

"I haven't got a lady."

Her eyes brightened with mischief.

"Don't get any ideas," he growled.

She smiled prettily. "Don't be so conceited. I could do way better—"

Damn. This was going all wrong. He had to get back on the right track. "Hey, I got hurt trying to save your—"

"All you did was get in the way. I could've handled Jeff—I've done it before."

Rafe took a deep, controlled breath. The little smart aleck had insulted him again, big time. And just when he had a yen for a bit of gratitude. He studied the way her pretty, kissable mouth kept smiling at him so flirtatiously. She thought she was really something.

She thought she was so rich and so pretty she could get away with any damn thing she wanted to. He had to keep his distance—emotionally, professionally—but just because she gave her old man a run for his money didn't mean she was going to do the same to him.

That's when Rafe caught the skinny brat roughly by the shoulders, yanking her up on her tiptoes, stretching her so close to his body that he could feel the heat of her again, that he could catch the sweet lavender smell of her. Half carrying her, half shoving her, he marched her toward the wall, his long legs striding forward into hers, forcing her to back up fast.

He liked the look of fright that flickered across her face when her shoulder blades touched brick and she knew she was trapped. "Not so fast, Skinny." His bronzed hand closed gently around her throat and twisted her pretty face to his. "Do you mean you've dated that bastard before, and you're dumb enough to sneak out with him again?"

"Who appointed you my guardian angel?"

No way could he answer that one, so he stared her down, satisfied when her dark eyes widened farther.

"What are you, crazy? Or are you just so hard up for a guy you'll go out with anyone?"

Something fragile and lonely came into her eyes that caught him off guard. "No... I could get anybody..."

"Because you're rich or because—"

She looked away but not before her stricken eyes had made him feel that her soul had reached out to his.

She caught her quivering lower lip with her teeth. When she let it go, her mouth was all wet and shiny.

For a long moment his gaze focused on her mouth.

Then a sudden tremor shook him.

She was so damned sexy. Which she obviously knew. But so damned stupid.

"Didn't your mama ever teach you not to tease guys?" he rasped, knowing he shouldn't hold her so close, knowing he was being sucked across some dangerous line. "Don't you know what could happen next time if you don't get lucky again? That guy can't hold his liquor—it was obvious he'd lost all control. I bet he's hurt other women."

When she tried to jerk free, Rafe's fingers tightened. "Listen to me!"

She glanced down at his bruising hands. "And you haven't ever hurt a woman?"

Rafe saw a little boy watching a man slam his mother onto the floor, screaming at her to take the cash, that she was trash and that he never wanted to see her or her son again. He saw the little boy putting his hands over his ears to shut out her sobs, dying inside when the door slammed and his father walked out forever.

He remembered the bruises on his mother's face. He remembered his father's parting words: "I despise you.

You are the last, the very last woman I would ever marry."

And he remembered the suitcase full of money that was lying open on the bed.

"No—I never hurt a woman," Rafe said aloud.

"Well, then... you'd better let go of me," she said quietly.

He relaxed his grip and inhaled a deep, slow breath. "Right." His voice came out low and muffled. "Look, I've spent a lot of years with a lot of rich lowlifes like your... friend Jeff. He's no good. Take this as a warning—you're going to get hurt if you don't start picking men more carefully."

"I've known Jeff a long time. He's part of my crowd."

"You need a new crowd then." Rafe eased his hands from her shoulders and backed out of her way.

He expected her to rush past him.

She stayed where she was.

"Maybe I do... need a new crowd, but I don't get many opportunities to make new friends," she said.

He didn't like it at all when she began studying him with new interest. Women hadn't chased him all his life for nothing. He knew that look. And it spelled trouble.

"Who are you?" she asked softly, her husky voice going through him like an electric shock. "What were you doing out here—alone in the dark?"

"It's kind of complicated. Why were you climbing that wall?"

"I was bored out of my mind and looking for some excitement," she answered in that low velvet tone.

"Well, I'll be damned. I was bored out of my mind, too."

"Maybe we can find some way to entertain each other," she said, swaying closer into his space, so that this time, he was the one who began backing away.

"Don't chicken out on me—hon," she whispered. "You're supposed to be a bad-boy biker, remember?"

"Right."

Her smiling lips seemed to beckon teasingly, heating Rafe's blood.

He had to fight to remember that he was a coolheaded professional, that he was her paid bodyguard—that he hated rich girls like her, on general principle.

But he badly wanted a taste of that kissable mouth. Just as badly as he wanted to banish the look of loneliness in her eyes. Not that he wouldn't have stayed cool.

If she hadn't licked her lips and gotten them all wet again.

If she hadn't reached up and crushed her mouth to his. Hard.

Then everything spun crazily out of control.

His cool professional brain shifted into neutral. His primitive male senses shifted into overdrive, and all he knew was a mindless, hormonal glory of the hot sweetness of her delicious mouth, tasting him, licking him. When her lips parted invitingly, he couldn't resist pushing his tongue inside her warm silken depths.

Clinging tighter to his wide shoulders, she moaned. At that muted, feminine sound, a wildness filled him, consumed him.

The brat was a wanton. And she wasn't as skinny as he'd thought. Maybe she was slim, but she was full-bosomed. And if ever a girl was asking for it—

One kiss and she'd pulled him into a furnace. No way could he stop then. Not with those velvet lips sliding across his mouth, his throat, not with her tongue flicking into his ear and setting him on fire.

He forgot who he was. Or who she was. No longer did it matter that she was rich and he was poor. Her hot mouth blurred all the bitter realities about their relationship. He was her paid bodyguard. She hated bodyguards, and he disliked spoiled rich girls.

He was breaking the rules of his chosen profession. He was breaking all the personal codes he lived by.

But nothing mattered. Nothing except the way her soft curves fit so perfectly into his long legs and hard-muscled thighs. His hands ruffled through the silken gold of her hair. He kissed her long and deeply until he felt her begin to tremble against him. In another minute—

It was a good thing she pushed him away when she did.

"You're a good kisser," she said breathlessly, smiling up at him. "You must've done that before."

He wasn't ready to admit to this fast conceited imp that kissing her had taken him a lot further than kissing any other woman ever had. Way too far.

"Yeah," he growled, his breath so harsh and rough he could barely speak. "A time or two. How about you, Skinny? I can tell you've been around the block a time or two."

"A time...or two," she agreed pertly, offhandedly, teasingly.

Hot, jolting anger made his blue eyes blaze as he thought of the other men who had already had her.

She flushed uneasily. "Couldn't you tell?"

"Look..." His voice was hard. "I don't want to know about all the other guys—"

"Does that mean you want to be my guy?"

Not in a million lifetimes! "You move fast," he said aloud. *Too fast.*

She was going to be hell on wheels to protect if she came on to other guys the way she came on to him.

"No, this is just happening fast. Don't you feel it?"

No—he had the situation under professional control. "Look—you kissed me, Skinny. Maybe I got a little excited, but it was purely sexual and a mistake."

"I don't think so."

Something sparkled from the ground. "Somehow I don't think your family would approve of me." He leaned down and carefully picked up the necklace Jeff had torn from her neck.

"So? What do they know? They love Jeff."

"He's rich," Rafe muttered. "He can afford to give you diamonds."

Rich and born on the right side of the sheets.

Rafe took her hand and dropped the sparkling necklace into it. He studied the gems glowing like white fire in her cupped hand. He knew he would never be able to afford even one piece of jewelry like that, even if he worked a lifetime. But to her, it was probably just another trinket.

He frowned, unaware that she was studying him as he avidly studied the diamonds. She snapped her hand shut, and when he looked at her, she smiled brightly. "I've got it—you're a thief!"

"A thief?" Furious, he froze. "I've never stolen a damn thing in my life."

"You don't have to yell. I didn't mean it as an insult."

"Look, I just work in your neighborhood."

"I don't care if you are a thief," she said, her eyes gleaming. "In fact . . . I like the idea."

It figured. She had sneaked out of her house with a drunk, and then come on to him like a house on fire. She was just the kind of nitwit who would see befriending a thief as a grand adventure.

She'd dealt the cards. His sixth sense told him only a fool would refuse to play such a good hand.

So she hated bodyguards, and she liked thieves. Who was he to judge? He was supposed to protect her, and to do that he had to stay close to her. Which was going to be difficult if they didn't hit it off.

If she wanted a thief, he'd be a thief.

"I figured it out when you were looking at those diamonds, and that's the only reason I can think of why someone like you would be lurking out here at two a.m."

"While you were figuring, how come you didn't figure me for a butler?"

She shook her head. "No way. Now, don't lie. I—I promise . . . I won't tell."

"If you want to think I'm some kind of Robin Hood...who takes from the rich and gives to the poor—me being the poor—you go right ahead, Skinny," he said with seeming reluctance.

"I knew it!" she sang, bobbing up and down on her bare tiptoes.

Then she reached up and traced her fingers along the hard chest muscles beneath his jacket. He caught her hand and held it still.

"Skinny, you're playing with fire."

"I know." Her eyes slanted up at him and grew hot and dark. "But I like it."

To a girl like her, he was the forbidden. He was someone to use—till she grew bored and needed some new more exciting form of entertainment.

Old bitterness rose in him, and without thinking he angrily grabbed her and brought his hard mouth brutally down on hers. Two could play the using game.

Not that she minded. Her arms wrapped around his neck. Her lips were eager, hot.

"Where's your getaway vehicle?" she asked a long time later when his anger was gone and he was too charged up by another unwanted emotion to deny her anything.

"You mean my motorcycle."

"No wonder you're wearing that awful jacket. That's great! I've never driven a motorcycle."

"*Driven?* Did you say *driven?*"

After she kissed him again and recharged all the right batteries, she demanded his key. "Take me to your hideout."

"If you have a lick of sense, you'll agree to meet me tomorrow, then climb back over that wall like a good girl."

When she shook her golden head, one of her dangling diamond clips flew out.

If she had a lick of sense, her father wouldn't have had to hire him.

"If my new bodyguard turns up tomorrow, I might not be able to get away," she said as Rafe leaned down and picked up her clip.

"My *hideout* it is, then," Rafe murmured ironically, rationalizing that maybe it wasn't such a bad idea. At least Mike would be home to protect *him*.

Rafe led her across the street to the bike he'd hidden in the shrubs. "Climb on," he ordered grimly when she hesitated. Then he got on behind her, and explained everything.

"I think I've got it figured out," she whispered as she buckled his helmet under her chin.

"Then let's get the hell out of here."

When she pressed too hard on the gas, the big bike bucked off the curb like a bronco lunging out of a chute. She screamed with laughter when he nearly fell off and had to grab her hard by the waist.

As they sped through the flying dark, her filmy skirts whipping his legs, he realized she was going to give him the ride of his life.

One

"**D**amn it!" Cathy hissed as she studied the reflection of her pale narrow face and huge dark eyes in the mirror. "You haven't got the courage God gave a mouse! What kind of mother is afraid of her own darling, six-year-old daughter?"

The humble shopkeeper selling fluorescent skulls in the market of the quaint, impoverished Mexican village—which one of the world's wealthiest women had improbably chosen as the perfect spot to bring up the diminutive whirlwind in question—would have agreed that Cathy had no reason to be afraid. Unless, however, she intended to cross the little girl. For Sadie, who was a pixie-faced angel as long as her mother gave her her way, had become something entirely different that afternoon in the market when her mother had said that horrid, two-letter word *no*. Or more specifically, "No, my sweet, darling *Gordita*, I'm afraid you cannot have one of those purple fluorescent skulls. I don't care if it glows in the dark!''

At *no,* the petite angel had frowned and chewed on her lip. At the words *you cannot have,* her cheeks had puffed out and turned tomato red. And when her mother had held firmly to the little hand and tried to coax her away, the child couldn't have yelled louder if a huge stake had been hammered through her heart. In the heat of this battle, a dozen fluorescent skulls had flown from the table and been smashed, and when Cathy had had to let go of Sadie's hand to pull money from her purse to pay the damages, Sadie had seized the biggest and grandest skull and galloped away with it as gleefully as a marauding bandit.

But Cathy was not thinking of that latest disastrous shopping spree as she turned away from her mirror. Nor was she worrying about her own disheveled appearance—for that was her norm.

The lopsided, butter yellow knot perched on top of her head looked as shaggy as a haystack. Her faded jeans were ragged. The rip above her right knee gaped open and showed way too much honey-toned skin and luscious thigh—especially when one considered she was supposed to at least try to look the part of the virtuous, grieving widow.

Except for the huge diamond on her left hand, Cathy never looked and never acted like one of the world's wealthiest heiresses. And until she had allowed Maurice Dumont the honor of placing that unwanted five-carat lump of ice on her finger, she had been the despair of her internationally famous, socialite mother and billionaire stepfather who were the brightest megastars in their jet-setting firmament. And if Cathy hadn't borne such a striking resemblance to her glamorous mother, all three might have believed that some madcap stork had mistakenly dropped the wrong baby down the chimney.

A little over six and a half years ago, the frustrating relationship between these fabled parents and their unsatisfactory daughter had sunk to an all-time low when Cathy had turned up pregnant—and naturally by the most unsuitable of seducers, that gorgeous brash bodyguard with a bad attitude and splendid tattooed biceps who had ordered them all about as arrogantly as if *he'd* been the billionaire.

Naturally nobody had thought it necessary to inform *him* that he held the dubious honor of being the unwanted sire to near royalty. Naturally Cathy had insisted on keeping the baby. Naturally her mother, who worried about appearances, had thought it best to rehire their old nurse, Pita, and build this beautiful house in Pita's remote Mexican mountain village far from the press's prying eyes, so the child could be raised secretly in one of the only places Cathy had ever been happy. And naturally Cathy's stepfather, who lied to everyone that he was a Mexican blueblood who could trace his ancestry back to El Cid and a Spanish king, found a way to get revenge against the treacherous seducer of his daughter.

Thankfully that terrible time was past. Armi had cleverly persuaded Cathy to come out of seclusion to dazzle Maurice. Cathy was once more the fabled family's darling, and Rafe Steele and the profound unhappiness the allure of his bronzed biceps had caused them were ancient history.

Or so Cathy thought as she stood in her bedroom, nervously twisting Maurice's huge ring round and round on her slender finger while she stared at her suitcases and contemplated her brilliant marriage and her difficult child with an uneasy emotion curiously akin to dread.

Her stomach tightened. What she had to do tonight was to try again to explain to Sadie that in less than two weeks she would have a wonderful new father, that she would be leaving this village where she'd grown up so happily, that she would be leaving her friends and her beloved Pita and Juanito forever, that her new home would be across a big ocean in a big castle in France where they would all live happily ever after.

Sadie, who was whimsical and highly imaginative and rather stubborn—that was an indulgent mother putting her little darling's stormy tantrums and cold-eyed sulks that could last for days mildly—hadn't exactly taken to the elegant Maurice Dumont on the two occasions he'd come to Mexico expressly to win her favor.

Indeed, with a pious air Sadie had insisted on giving all the gorgeous stuffed animals he'd brought her to the poor village children; she'd pouted and then pretended to sneeze, turning her cheek away every time he'd tried to kiss it, saying she was afraid he'd get a sniffle; she'd refused to stay in any room where he happened to be; and Cathy still couldn't let herself remember the family of wiggling iguanas Sadie had stuffed into Maurice's suitcase after she'd found her mother and Maurice kissing and been shown the huge engagement ring and told about the wedding.

Sadie, who loved pageants and costumes of all varieties, had refused to be a flower girl, and she had threatened to do something absolutely horrid if Cathy forced her to come to the wedding. So, tonight Cathy was troubled about how exactly she would convince Sadie that they were all going to be so frightfully happy in their fairy-tale castle, when she herself—

Enough procrastinating. If she wasn't going to pack all the party dresses her mother had stipulated on her long list of what she was to bring, she'd better deal with Sadie.

Cathy went over to the balcony door and shuddered at the sight of the black mountain looming against a glowing sky. The mountain reminded her as nothing else could of how impossible it was to control Sadie. The soaring peaks that looked so impregnable were dangerously riddled with ancient silver mines, and Sadie, who was fascinated by them because she imagined ghosts lived in them, had been strictly forbidden to go near them.

A golden moon was rising in a darkening sky. But Cathy barely noticed. She was thinking of the crumbling tunnels that snaked like a maze for miles deep into the mountain—in fact, all the way to the other side. She was remembering with horror the July afternoon when Sadie and Juanito had vanished and all that could be found of them was one of Sadie's red polka dot ribbons by the entrance of a tunnel. For two terrifying days Cathy had nearly gone out of her mind while the villagers searched the tunnels and shafts. Then Sadie and Juanito had cheerfully emerged on the other side of the mountain with a bag full of food and candles, saying the adventure would have been grand if it hadn't been for the bats.

Cathy looked across her own red-tiled roofs and the high walls dripping with ivy that surrounded her lovely house and patios to the humbler corrugated roof of Pita's bright blue house across the narrow alley. Sadie was playing on Pita's patio.

In the morning, Cathy would be leaving the village. If she didn't make Sadie listen to her tonight, there wouldn't be another chance. At this very moment, her wedding guests, family and friends were flying in from all parts of the world and congregating at her parents' world-famous hacienda, Casa Tejas, in the valley at the base of the mountain to celebrate her marriage.

Her mother had planned endless parties and dances for the next two weeks, and the groom himself would be arriving in less than a week. That was when Cathy planned to sneak Maurice back to the village to see Sadie. Thus, Cathy had to find a way to convince Sadie to at least treat him politely.

As Cathy silently walked outside and descended the stairs that wound down to her walled courtyard, a mariachi band in the plaza began to play the one love song she would have paid them anything not to play.

Her luminous dark eyes widened. Her sweet face tensed. The wonderful, damnable music sent a bittersweet pang through her. For once, long ago, Rafe had stood under another balcony and serenaded her with that song.

She'd already been madly in love with him. How thrilled she had been by the slow, curling grin that had lit his lean dark features. He'd been dressed up like Elvis that night in his awful biker's jacket, and he had sung her favorite song pretending he was a Mexican Elvis, perfectly mimicking the great star's husky baritone in heavily accented gringo-Spanish. Then he'd sung "Love me Tender" and stripped a long red silk scarf from around his neck and tossed it to her before he'd kissed her.

Cathy sank against an ivy-covered column. Her hand fluttered to the golden heart-shaped locket Rafe had given her, which she told herself she wore only for Sadie's sake.

The column was cold against her flushed skin, but all she felt was a hot current of dark and undeniable passion for the man who had used her.

Dear God. Her fingers shook as she fumbled with the locket, taking the key out and pressing it against her left breast before slowly putting it back.

Rafe had been nothing more than a paid bodyguard who'd wanted to get laid and make a fast buck or two if he could.

She'd been happier thinking he was a thief.

But what he'd been above all else was a liar.

She'd grown up rich and protected by paid companions. She'd been so starved for real love that she'd been an easy conquest for him. All he'd wanted was to use her for sex, so he could negotiate a bigger payoff from Armi.

He hadn't been the first to pretend he cared when all he was after was money. Her best friend in high school had sold a story about her to a newspaper that specialized in sensational stories about celebrities. It was just that Rafe had so convincingly acted the part he'd played, Cathy had really trusted him.

Her hand fell to her side. Slowly she began twisting Maurice's diamond, squeezing her hand into it so tightly it cut into her palm.

Would she never be free of Rafe Steele?

Sadie, Cathy thought desperately. She had to find Sadie.

Only Sadie was a force dynamic enough to dispel her fear of Rafe's ghost.

"Mommy! Mommy!" Sadie shrieked from inside Pita's house, jumping up at the first faint groan of the loose board on the sagging porch.

A heavy clay pot shattered against the dirt floor inside.

"Ouch! Pita! *Se cayó!*" It fell!

"*No te preocupes, Gordita.*" Do not worry, little fatty.

Pita's kindly voice sounded far away, as if it came from the kitchen, and Cathy, who wanted to talk to her daughter alone, decided to let Pita worry about whatever was broken.

Stick-thin and hyperactive at six, Sadie had acquired the nickname *Gordita* when she had been a fat, placid baby, a few brief months cut short when she pulled herself up at seven months and began toddling. Pita and Cathy regarded that idyll with their little *Gordita* as the lull before the storm.

Cathy heard racing footsteps—Sadie never walked. Then the door was flung open so hard it banged twice against the crumbling cinder-block wall. And the dynamo, a skinny hoyden in a witch hat and trailing black gown stuck together with pins, stood bobbing up and down on her tiptoes. The elf smiled engagingly up at Cathy. "Come see what we're making!"

Sadie, who adored make-believe, especially costumes, was carrying a basket of marigolds.

Marigolds—

Cempasúchil flowers the Indians called these dazzling blossoms, which were reputed by the superstitious to have the power to attract the spirits of the dead.

Indeed, the plump fluffy marigolds gave off a powerful aromatic scent. Indeed, they did seem to glow with a special light.

Cathy felt a twinge of alarm as she realized that the approaching holiday everyone in the village was preparing for would occur the very day she planned to bring Maurice to see her daughter.

"Sadie, would you please come outside—"

Instead of obeying her mother, Sadie mashed her hat down and spun around faster than a dervish, sending pins and marigolds flying everywhere.

"Stop! Stop! You're making a mess," Cathy said, but with an indulgent smile. With an effort she forced herself to be sterner. "You're going to make yourself sick! You're losing all your marigolds!"

Sadie stopped instantly, but only because of the marigolds and because she was too dizzy to continue. "I wanted you to see how big and fat the skirt is," the child said. "Pita made it for me for Halloween and for *El Día de los Muertos,* too."

Cathy's second twinge of alarm was much stronger. Her faint motherly smile tightened at the thought of the pagan festival.

The Day of the Dead was a magical, two-day Mexican holiday that began every first of November, and turned their normally quiet village into a madhouse. The holiday was considered a sacred time, when departed spirits were welcomed back to earth by the faithful to drink and eat and visit their families.

"Pita made the costume out of one of Lupe's old black witch dresses, so that makes it specially magic—like the marigolds—cause Lupe was a real witch!"

Another sharper twinge struck in the center of Cathy's chest as she reconsidered the basket of marigolds and their magic powers to attract the good spirits back to their family's homes.

Lupe Sanchez, Pita's famous mother, had been dead ten years. Cathy remembered her as a withered old crone filled with self-importance about her reputation as the most celebrated witch and *curandera*—spell caster—in the whole state of Jalisco. She knew Lupe had laid a terrible guilt trip on Pita for not gaining an equally grand name in the same "profession."

Now, Cathy didn't believe for a second that stern old Lupe had ever really been a witch, and Cathy most certainly did not wish Sadie's head to be filled with such foolishness, either. But, no matter how Cathy begged Pita not to talk about witches, Pita and everyone else in the village believed too deeply in them not to pass on to her adored child just a few of their favorite stories about Pita's notorious mother.

"Come outside, darling," Cathy insisted more sharply.

Sadie bounced backward. "No! I'm helping Pita build her altar so that Lupe can come back and eat tamales and green salsa!"

This was too much!

"There are no such things as witches! I don't care what Pita says, ghosts don't really come back! And they certainly don't eat tamales and salsa!"

"Pita doesn't say that!"

"Good, I'm glad that's settled, now—"

Cathy stopped, for Sadie's blazing blue eyes didn't look the least bit settled. And indeed, they unsettled Cathy, too, because they reminded her too much of Rafe's eyes and the way they had blazed on that terrible last afternoon, when he'd saved Armi's life and she'd found out *he* was her bodyguard. Indeed, the striking resemblance the blond pixie bore to her odious father upset Cathy so much, she began to shake.

"Pita doesn't say ghosts eat! She says they just suck all the good stuff out of the food—" Sadie pursed her lips and made a horrid slurping sound just like she did when she inhaled long strings of gooey spaghetti. "Like that!"

The vision of a wizened, black-shawled Lupe slurping spaghetti was too absurd to consider.

Suddenly, Cathy was glad she was getting married. Sadie had reached the age where she needed more than dear superstitious Pita or the street-smart orphan Juanito could provide. Sadie needed a father to discipline her, as well as the wonderful advantages a man like Maurice could give her.

As Maurice's adopted daughter, she would be expected to conduct herself as a well-bred young lady. Naturally she would attend the finest French schools. Cathy imagined sweet, friendly children and loving teachers, sharing and learning together in sunlit classrooms.

Fortunately, this dazzling moment of motherly insight was not marred by the memory of her own dreadful experiences at a highly reputed Swiss boarding school. Fortunately, the memory of spending long lonely hours in solitary confinement for the slightest infraction of Madame Bremond's cruel rules was buried too deeply for her to recall quite so swiftly. But Cathy, who had also been a skinny, pixie-like child, had been too lively to endure such a rigid environment happily. She had spent those miserable hours when she'd been isolated from the others writing her glamorous mother letter after letter, begging her to come and take her away because everybody spoke French and despised her and thought her too common to play with because she was an American. And her beautiful, partying mother had been briefly amused by the passion in those letters, saying lightly to a friend over an expensive Parisian lunch, "She will adjust."

But Cathy's mother had been wrong. Cathy made friends with the janitor's son and was expelled for sneaking off to play with him.

Now Cathy was brightening at the prospect of her daughter's grand future and was in no mood to dwell on the fact that she had never been able to fit into high society or make friends with anyone who seemed phony.

When Sadie made an even louder slurping sound and was about to make another, Cathy took her firmly by the hand and led her toward the hand-carved chairs on the porch.

"Darling, those are perfectly marvelous ghost sounds. But I really don't care to argue about whether ghosts eat or suck their food—I—I have the most wonderful news."

At Cathy's coaxing motherly smile, Sadie scowled and yanked her hand loose.

Cathy sat down with seeming casualness and pulled Sadie's smaller chair closer to her own. "Here. Why don't you sit here beside me—"

Instead of obeying, Sadie marched to the end of the porch and squatted grumpily on the floor like her Indian friend Juanito and began to tear the petals off a puffy marigold. "I've got some good news, too," the little girl whispered sullenly, letting the petals fall into the basket.

As Sadie ripped at the flowers, Cathy's stomach tightened. Did the child have some special radar that made her sense her mother was about to try to discuss Maurice again?

"I wish you would stop doing that!" Cathy blurted out.

Sadie's fingers tore the flowers with even greater vengeance. "Pita needs these petals to make a path from the cemetery to show Lupe the way home."

Cathy swallowed and decided on a less direct approach. "Why . . . why don't you tell me your news first, darling?"

Sadie's fingers paused over a half-shredded flower. Her pixie features grew still. For once she didn't rush. After a long time, she finally began in a small strangled tone, "Pita says . . . that maybe Lupe will bring my real daddy this year when she comes . . ."

Sadie's wistful voice seemed to die away. Which was just as well, because Cathy couldn't have borne another word. Almost never did she speak to Sadie about Rafe, but the sorrow in Sadie's voice was too great to ignore.

"No!" Cathy cried fiercely, springing up and rushing to Sadie. Cathy sank to her knees. "Oh, my poor little darling—I can't bear for you to go on thinking, to go on hoping—"

Very gently Cathy pulled her child into her arms, and as she did, the pointy witch hat fell off.

Tenderly Cathy smoothed the stray golden tangles out of her little girl's baby-fine hair. "My precious *Gordita*, he won't ever come."

Sadie was very still. "How do you know?"

"I—I just know."

They clung to each other, sharing the deep dark silence of the night. Then the wind caught the witch hat, and it began to roll away.

Sadie cried, "My hat!" and wriggled free to get it.

Sadie's hands were quick and jerky as she mashed it back on her head, no longer caring that she was crumpling it.

"Sadie, please, believe me—he can't ever—"

Sadie's ice blue eyes seemed to look through her. "Mommy, why did God make my daddy die?"

The pinched pixie face underneath the tall black hat blurred.

Cathy would have done anything to spare her child such anguish, but how could she, when she had caused it?

"Sadie, I don't really know why any of the things that have happened . . . happened. That's just . . . life."

"Then tell me about how my daddy was so big and tall," she pleaded softly. "About how he was a Texan and he talked like this, 'How-d-y, ma'am.'" Charmingly she drew out the cliché words with a dramatic, childish flourish. Sadie was immensely talented when it came to languages and copying accents. She could mimic Maurice to a T.

"You must have been watching some cowboy Westerns," Cathy said.

"I reckon I—I—I have been, ma'am."

Cathy almost smiled. "The drawl is a bit overdone. And Rafe never said howdy or called me ma'am."

No, he had called her Skinny. Not that he'd meant the huskily purred nickname—rolling off his drawling tongue as sexily and slowly as liquid velvet—as an insult.

"And he wore a great big cowboy hat and boots?"

"The night I met him, he was wearing black leather and riding a motorcycle."

"That's even better."

"Yes . . . it was." Cathy caught herself. She was supposed to be selling Sadie on Maurice.

But the child so wanted her to conjure up images of Rafe, and somehow, talking about him with his daughter tonight wasn't nearly as hard as usual.

"Most of the time, he wore cowboy hats and boots," Cathy said softly.

But not when he made love. He'd always been careful to take care of his hat and she'd been careful about his boots.

Sadie got up and tiptoed toward her mother. Reaching up, she reverently touched the locket. "And he gave you this?"

Cathy nodded.

"Because he loved you?"

For an instant, Cathy thought she might fly to pieces. Once she had believed that.

"Yes." Strange, how her single word sounded so utterly calm.

Her child's seeking fingertips were soft and warm and loving against her throat, the same way Rafe's had been when he'd first fastened the locket there.

"And you wear it because you still love him?"

There was a wealth of hope, such a profound belief in undying love in that small voice. Suddenly, Cathy felt old, old beyond her years as she gazed blankly down at her daughter.

The lies. The wretched, wretched lies. Why did there seem to be so many of them? And the biggest lie of all was that Sadie's father couldn't possibly come back from the grave with Lupe.

And the reason he couldn't was because he wasn't dead.

No! The lying lowlife who'd pretended to love her to make his own job easier was very much alive. He'd taken money from Armi and used it to start his own international security business with Mike. And Rafe had made quite a name for himself protecting executives and celebrities and rescuing Americans held hostage in dangerous countries.

So much of a name that Rafe was a wanted man in Mexico, because it was widely believed that he'd broken into a Mexican prison three years ago. Supposedly, he'd handcuffed himself to a famous drug lord, Hernando Guillén, who'd been wanted for murder in the States—dragged him across the border and handed him over to the Houston cops. After Guillén was sentenced to death and the U.S. refused his extradition to Mexico, the incident had caused international repercussions.

When Armi had gone to Manuel in a rage over Rafe's unprofessional romance with Cathy, Manuel had sympathized, saying he'd had a similar problem several years back when he'd sent Rafe to Peru after his daughter, Consuelo, who had run off with a freedom fighter. When Consuelo had refused to leave, Rafe had handcuffed her to himself and dragged her out of the jungle against her will. One week handcuffed to him in the jungle, and she'd come back madly in love—and no longer with her guerrilla soldier.

Manuel had philosophically held the view that Rafe had gotten both women safely through dangerous situations. He'd pointed out that Rafe had single-handedly tackled the hired hit man who'd attempted to shoot Armi at that political fund-raiser in Memorial Park in Houston.

Cathy sighed. This very moment Rafe was probably protecting some other woman; probably making love to her. Cathy couldn't bear to think about it. But there was no way she could tell her daughter the unsavory truths about her unscrupulous father. It was better that she believed in her fantasies.

"Yes, in a way...I still love him," Cathy said, hugging her daughter close again. And at that, Sadie became very quiet and still, and, clutching the locket as though it were her greatest treasure, she slipped her other hand around her mother's neck and kissed her.

Cathy remembered the night Rafe had given her the locket.

"Did you steal it?" she'd asked breathlessly, hopefully.

"No," he'd said, his voice deep and husky. "It was my

mother's." There had been a heart-stopping silence. "It was a gift from my father to my mother."

"I—I won't ever take it off."

Then he'd crushed his mouth to hers and pulled her down on top of him on the bed.

But Cathy couldn't tell Sadie that.

"He would be so proud of you, my darling *Gordita,*" Cathy murmured at last. "So very proud."

Mother and daughter clung, Cathy feeling freer somehow because she'd survived a conversation about Rafe; Sadie fantasizing about the big tall cowboy-father she would have given anything to know.

Later, Cathy would think it odd that Rafe, who had torn her life apart and made her an exile from her family for so long, had brought her this rare shining moment of closeness with her daughter.

But no moment, however rare and special, lasts forever, and all too soon Sadie picked up her basket and was back to shredding marigolds.

"Can I go show Juanito my witch costume?" Sadie asked after she plucked the last petal from a marigold and tossed another naked stem carelessly onto the others strewn about the floor.

Juanito was a seven-year-old orphan who Pita and several Indian housewives fed. His grandfather had been a silver miner and then a notorious bandit. Juanito was so smart and adorable the whole pueblo loved him. The boy slept wherever there was a spare bed, and when he couldn't find a bed, it was rumored that he slept in the mines.

Cathy knew she should say no. She knew she should make her daughter clean up the messy pile of stems. Just as she knew she should find some way to talk to Sadie about Maurice.

But Sadie's big blue eyes were as imploring as Rafe's, and as Cathy bent down and began to gather the stems, all she could bring herself to say was yes.

Two

"Pita?"

Cathy's voice held a crushed note from having failed yet again to talk to Sadie about Maurice.

"Aquí, mi vida. En la cocina," Pita called welcomingly from the kitchen, which was redolent of the scent of tamales and green salsa.

Cathy hesitated inside the door, her gaze wandering in the darkness. A sliver of moonlight slanted eerily through a large crack in one wall and illuminated a huge altar. Three tiers of boxes had been draped with white satin.

Cathy pulled a string under a bare bulb. The dirt floor had been swept, the scarred tables and crucifix immaculately dusted. A plastic box of pins and scraps of black fabric were stacked on top of an ancient sewing machine. A small pair of scissors lay beside Pita's larger ones; Sadie's dragon stool had been pulled next to Pita's.

Once when Cathy had asked Pita how she had the patience to sew or cook with Sadie around, Pita had replied, "From raising you, *Flaquita*."

Little Skinny. The Spanish nickname always disturbed her, for it was too close to Rafe's.

Pita's house might be humble, even dilapidated, but it felt more like home than any of the palaces Cathy had grown up in. And the status Pita had in this village as the daughter of the legendary Lupe was grander than any king's. Indians from other villages still made pilgrimages to pay homage to her and to her mother's house, which was practically a shrine.

When Pita had refused to move into the fine apartment Cathy had built for her beside her own house, Cathy had almost been glad. This beloved little shack had always been Cathy's refuge whenever her own life had gone wrong.

Cathy studied the huge altar Pita was carefully building. Beneath Lupe's stern photograph, Lupe's famous diary that dealt with witchcraft lay open to a yellowed page, upon which she had inscribed her golden rule in Spanish.

To temper with the fate of a man causes a chain of events to be set into motion over which no one will have ultimate control.

On another, Lupe had written merely three words: *Nothing is impossible.*

Next to the diary were the empty black Oaxagan vases Pita would fill with marigolds, and a stack of white beeswax candles. On a lower shelf, a row of sugar skulls grinned up at her.

Cathy flipped through the diary until she came to the last page. The ink was so light it seemed to have soaked into the ancient parchment, and Cathy had to squint to make out the dim script.

At first she thought it was some sort of recipe.

When she bent over it and read the title, her hands began to tremble.

No...

Yes, a silent voice boomed.

Just for an instant the room seemed to darken. The words seemed to leap off the page and grow larger, glowing a sickly greenish yellow. Lupe's photograph seemed to gleam with the same iridescent light.

Cathy shivered and withdrew her hand from the page as if burned. It wasn't a recipe at all.

But a spell.

For true love.

Cathy's shaky fingertips found the locket at her throat. She felt her quick, jerky heartbeat.

She thought of Maurice, and the long years of her life stretching before her seemed to promise no brightness.

If only...

Why did she have to remember riding on a motorcycle through a warm humid night, bronzed male hands clasped tightly around her narrow waist as her white chiffon skirts flew all over a hunk's black jeans?

For a long moment, she just stood there in the quiet, gripped by the wildest longing she had ever known and a strange panic that the rest of her life, fairy-tale perfect as it might seem on the surface, would lack passion and adventure—and, most of all, love.

Then the words in the diary grew smaller and dimmer, the ink seeming to fade back into the page. Cathy tore her hand from the locket and drew herself up rigidly. She tried to smooth a wayward butter yellow tendril out of her eyes, but more hair tumbled down from her top-knot.

Such dreams had brought her only heartbreak. Maybe it was better not to love so deeply. Maybe then she wouldn't be hurt so deeply. She saw herself being strengthened by Maurice's love, not torn apart as she had been by Rafe's.

Besides, who could take the spell of a mean old Indian woman seriously just because she'd been clever enough to trick ignorant villagers into believing she was a witch?

At that thought, the dirt floor seemed to rumble, and a violent red glare filled the room. A strange furious heat burned through Cathy. It was as if she stood before a blazing fire and was in real danger of being roasted alive.

In terror, Cathy's gaze flew back to Lupe's photograph, which still seemed to glow with that iridescent light. The black hair was parted severely in the middle; her stern Indian features and high cheekbones would have seemed ordinary had her intense black eyes not held Cathy's almost hypnotically.

Dear God... Was she going crazy from the strain of her impending wedding?

The hair on Cathy's neck arched and she felt oddly cold, oddly warm—and truly frightened that there really might be something to all this, that she really might have made Lupe angry by doubting her power.

Cathy tried to reassure herself that she *was* crazy, that Lupe was dead, that there was no such thing as white magic.

But Lupe Sanchez had convinced everyone who had ever known her that there was such a thing and that she was the supreme mistress of it.

The villagers had revered her even as they had been terrified of her. Suddenly, Cathy remembered the way there had always been someone in Lupe's kitchen whispering quietly, seeking the old woman's help. Mothers of sick children, wives whose husbands had strayed, wives who wanted to reform their husbands who drank too much and beat them—they had all come to Lupe and bought her potions and powders, believing in the power of her spells.

They still came to Lupe's daughter, and dear Pita tried valiantly to live up to her mother's past glories. But poor Pita's spells had a tendency to go haywire.

Not that the villagers had any complaints about the sick children, for Pita was talented with children. But Pita had never wanted to knuckle under to a macho husband, and she had refused to marry—saying that marriage for a poor woman in Mexico was slavery. Thus, Pita never had much luck when it came to mixing magic and men.

The wives who bought Pita's potions because they wanted to reform their straying husbands all too frequently ran off to Mexico City with handsome young lovers. And there was the truly disturbing story of the very timid and long-abused seamstress Elsa Pacheco, who had come to Pita and paid for a magic potion to change her drunken lout, Abelardo, who beat her and their children every night, into a model husband.

Pita had taken Elsa's money and dutifully concocted what she promised was her most powerful potion. Pita had instructed Elsa to pour it into the unsuspecting Abelardo's pulque. But that very night, after swigging the pulque laced with Pita's potion, the abusive Abelardo had come home even drunker and meaner than ever.

Wielding his knife, he'd chased all seven of the little Pachecos out of the house into the cornfield, even nicking a piece off the oldest son's right ear. Then Abelardo had beaten his wife and made brutal drunken love to her before passing out like a dying bull on top of her.

Bruised and beaten, Elsa had become so desperate—because Pita's spell had only made things worse—that she, a virtuous Catholic, succumbed to the temptation of stealing a single consoling sip of Abelardo's pulque. After draining the second bottle, she'd called the seven little Pachecos inside and ordered them to help her sew all the serapes they owned around Abelardo's corpulent body until he was tightly sewn into his bed and more helpless than a prisoner in a straitjacket.

The next morning when he'd awakened with a roar and screamed for Elsa to let him go, she had quietly picked up the heavy iron she used to press her seams and beaten him until he'd wept for mercy, until he'd sworn between choking sobs to never touch pulque again if only Elsa would promise the same. And after that, although everyone knew that Pita's spell had failed so abysmally, Pita somehow attracted even more clients. And Abelardo, who never drank pulque again, became the most docile and henpecked of husbands.

For one moment longer, Lupe's portrait remained iridescent, and the air suddenly grew eerily cold and damp. For one moment longer, Lupe's black eyes burned into Cathy.

And Cathy, who couldn't bear to hurt anyone's feelings, knelt down repentantly before the portrait just in case.

"Oh, Lupe," Cathy whispered. "I'm sorry. I meant no disrespect. It's not your fault I don't believe in witches. I...I almost wish I could. I wish life were that simple."

Cathy felt the floor tremble again. The sugar skulls clattered ominously.

Something cold and still seemed to caress her cheek. *Anything is possible,* came a silent voice from behind her. Cathy jumped back from the altar. For a second there, it really had seemed as if Lupe's invisible spirit had been there.

Then the floor shook again, and Cathy sprang up wildly, screaming for Pita.

"Momentito!" Just a minute!

At the sound of Pita's warm, loving voice, Cathy felt reassured, almost back to normal.

Her short, fat coffee-colored nurse waddled out of the kitchen, wiping her hands on her white apron. "Did you feel the baby earthquakes?"

"Oh—"

Baby earthquakes. There were constant tremors in this region. Usually they didn't mean much.

Still, Cathy felt so scared that for a long while her tongue seemed stuck to the roof of her mouth.

Finally, when she could talk, she said, "Pita, your altar seems to get bigger every year."

"Like me," Pita said, grinning, patting her apron, not in the least ashamed of her rotund figure. "I have to build it." She approached the altar and picked up her mother's picture. "You know how everybody admired her."

"I—I . . . know."

"Everyone always comes here this time of year when she comes back . . . to pray for her help."

"Uh, I'd rather not talk about—"

"She's been dead a long time, but they still believe in her powers far more than they do in mine," Pita said, a little jealously.

"Oh, don't feel bad," Cathy implored. "You're wonderful in your own way."

"She had so much talent and grandeur—she couldn't understand why I wasn't as talented."

"My famous, talented mother doesn't understand me any better."

"Lupe tried so hard to teach me, but the spells—they are so complicated." Pita brightened. "And then I always feel the need to add a little something extra—just to see what will happen."

"Which is what makes you a wonderful cook! You are so creative!"

"But adding things to spells doesn't work the way it does with recipes," Pita murmured.

"Well, you never can tell. Maybe you'll come up with the greatest spell that ever was! Maybe it'll be so great, Lupe will turn green in her grave."

"I wish!" But Pita said this so sadly, Cathy knew she was dwelling on all her failures. "I'll have to try harder. But things have a way of going *loco* when I try something new."

"Oh, Pita, I wish you—" Cathy stopped herself, suddenly feeling depressed and uncertain. Where was she going with this? She didn't believe in witchcraft. But she loved Pita too much to hurt her by saying so.

"What's bothering you, my *Flaquita?*"

Cathy came into Pita's arms. "I'm going to miss you, Pita."

"You will have your new husband, your new life."

Maurice's castles were so far away. And they were too like Armi's faux palaces. Somehow, Cathy didn't think Maurice was going to allow her to come back to this village and her beloved Pita very often, and Pita had been the only person who'd ever seemed to genuinely love her just for herself. That was why Cathy had brought her child here, to this simple impoverished village, and tried to give her daughter the kind of warm loving childhood she had never had herself.

For no reason at all, Pita's words brought tears, and then Cathy was blurting out the truth to the one person in all the world she could really talk to.

"Oh, Pita. It's everything. I can't talk to Sadie about Maurice. I... Pita, I want to be in love, the way I was with— I want to be in love with Maurice."

"There there, my little *Flaquita*. You told me you did love him—"

"I told you so I would believe it myself!"

"All the newspapers say—"

"They say what my mother and Armi tell them to say! And it isn't that Maurice isn't good and right for me, because he is!"

"Then what's wrong?"

"I want to love him in the same wild way I loved Rafe."

Pita's dark eyes shifted to a strange-looking jumble of teetering boxes partially swathed in raggedly cut remnants of white satin.

"Did you see the altar our little *Gordita* built?"

When Cathy turned, she saw a smaller altar leaning drunkenly against Pita's.

"She made it in honor of Rafe," Pita said. "She's been struggling so hard on it. I didn't tell you because—"

As if in a daze, Cathy moved toward it. Three badly balanced boxes were only partially covered with scraps of satin. On the bottom box Sadie had laid out her dearest possessions. In the center, displayed as proudly as if it were an emperor's crown jewel, was her latest ill-gotten treasure.

The purple fluorescent skull gleamed up at Cathy with dark triumph. Beside it in the small golden frame Sadie had demanded last week, was a picture of Rafe on his motorcycle.

So this was why Sadie had been such a little monster in the market.

The photograph—Cathy's only photograph of Rafe, for Armi had found the others and destroyed them—was supposed to be locked away in her jewelry box. And Sadie wasn't supposed to know it even existed.

Cathy's hand went to her locket, where she kept the key.

Somehow the little minx, who constantly sifted through all of Cathy's possessions and denied that she ever did so, had taken the key and stolen the picture, too.

But Cathy didn't dwell on Sadie's innumerable crimes, rather on the poignant reason behind them.

Her poor darling was desperately lonely for a father.

"Oh, Pita," Cathy said, collapsing before the tiny altar. With a shudder, she touched the garish purple glitter of the skull's arching eyebrows. "I have to marry Maurice. And the sooner the better. Sadie needs a father so much. I know that, in time, she'll come to accept Maurice."

"But if you don't love him yourself—"

"Oh, Pita, if only there really was such a thing as witchcraft. If only *you* had Lupe's talent and really could concoct a spell and make me fall in love with Maurice."

Pita stiffened, drawing back with wounded pride and profound sorrow.

Cathy realized instantly what she had done. "Oh, Pita. I'm so sorry. I should never have compared you to—I didn't mean—"

"Everybody always thinks Lupe is better—even you," Pita said in a small, pain-filled voice.

There was an awful, frozen silence. They both felt terrible, cut off from each other.

Too late, Cathy realized that her own pain had blinded her and made her thoughtlessly cruel.

No simple apology would suffice.

It was one thing for Pita to put herself and her talents down, but Cathy knew that it was quite another matter for someone else to do it. One wrong remark, one joke that she was a disappointment compared to her mother— and the normally jolly Pita would turn gloomy for days.

"Oh, Pita, I didn't mean it. You know that I didn't. I don't even believe in—"

"You did," Pita said glumly. "And you're right. I have no talent. I'm just a pitiful fraud. My spells never work. Remember the Pachecos. Who am I trying to fool?"

Slowly Cathy went to Pita, but when she tried to put her arms around the woman to comfort her, Pita shrugged free.

"Pita, please...please forgive me. I can't bear the thought of leaving tomorrow, knowing I've hurt you."

Pita's wounded gaze flickered past Cathy to her mother's stern photograph, which had gone iridescent again. "Nobody's ever believed in me. Especially not my mother... and I tried so hard. I—I still try."

"I believe in you, Pita. I've always believed in you. If it hadn't been for you, I would have had a truly miserable childhood."

Still, Pita hesitated. Finally, she gulped in a breath and spoke. "Then will you let me try to show, both you and Mother, you're all wrong?"

"I already know how wrong I was."

"No. I wasn't born the daughter of the great Lupe Sanchez for nothing," she said with a touch of Lupe's old arrogance. "If I dabble with my mother's potion for true love, will you give it to Maurice and take it yourself when you bring him back to see Sadie?"

Cathy thought potions were ridiculous. But she would have agreed to anything to make Pita feel better.

"Of course, I will, Pita."

Pita's black eyes gleamed with sudden inspiration as she marched across the room and picked up her mother's diary. "For once in my life, I'll show her. And I'll show you, too, Cathy. I'm going to make a spell that will turn the world upside down."

Cathy remembered the henpecked Abelardo and felt just the faintest qualm. The dirt floor beneath her feet trembled.

"Just another baby earthquake," Pita said on her way to the kitchen with the diary tucked against her plump bosom.

"Pita—maybe you shouldn't get too carried away. Now remember, all I want is to fall in love."

"I promise you, on the conceited soul of my esteemed mother—who, as you know, was the greatest witch and *curandera* in all of Jalisco—that you will fall in love. Madly, impossibly in love. And it will be even better than the first time."

Lupe Sanchez's photograph began to shake. Her whole altar rattled dangerously.

Cathy screamed, but Pita, her good humor entirely restored, smiled and said again, "Don't worry. It's just another baby earthquake."

Three

He was crazy to be here—suicidal to have driven so far into Mexico when the country alone was enough to make him paranoid.

Rafe reached involuntarily into his shirt pocket for his cigarettes before he remembered he'd quit six months ago.

Damn!

He replaced his hand on the steering wheel and drove with one eye on the road and the other looking over his shoulder. He was worried about a hell of a lot more than his new truck.

This whole thing could be just another setup to lure him across the border.

No way could the blue-eyed brat in the fuzzy snapshot Manuel had sent him really be his!

No way did Rafe want to have anything to do with the rich, half-baked screwball who'd nearly destroyed him.

After several bad years, Mike's and his business was really starting to fly. The last thing he needed was trouble like Cathy, who had had a peculiar knack for turning his life upside down. And she'd damn sure thrown him to the wolves when the heat was on.

The wolves being one very big bad wolf—Armi Calderon.

When a billion dollars had leaned on him, Rafe had felt it. And Armi had done a hell of a lot more than lean. He'd smashed. He'd pulverized.

Rafe, who prided himself on his tough-guy image, was secretly ashamed that he still had nightmares about the night he'd gotten drunk after Cathy had walked out on him. So blind drunk and professionally careless, he'd been easy pickings for Armi's four goons when he'd staggered out of his favorite bar. They tackled him from behind and dragged him into a dark alley. When he'd refused Armi's business proposition, Armi had ordered them to kick in his ribs.

Rafe had been sobbing like a baby, saying he'd take the money, when Armi had finally called them off. Then the rich bastard had just stood there in his three-piece suit and smiled down at Rafe groveling and writhing in the dirt. Finally, Armi had knelt and in a deadly soft voice said how his favorite dish in all the world was the American hamburger. Then Armi had taken out a monogrammed handkerchief and cleaned the blood off Rafe's mouth as gently as he might have tended a baby. But as he'd risen slowly, he'd said, "You drunken, two-bit, cheap piece of trash—if you ever cross me again or come near my stepdaughter, I'll let them turn you into hamburger."

Armi had flung an enormous wad of cash down into the blood and grime, along with the photographs he'd shredded that Cathy had taken of Rafe. Armi had pivoted on his heel and walked off, stopping at the end of the alley. "That's all you'll ever get out of me." Then very softly, very gently, he whispered, "Your life is my thank-you for saving my life."

Armi Calderon wanted people to think he came from class. And most people thought anybody with that kind of money was class. But the truth was he came from the gutter. He'd gotten rich fast because he was smart and mean. Because he was a bully who was very good at buying powerful people. Six and a half years ago, he'd enjoyed crushing Rafe like a bug. Rafe knew Armi would take personal pleasure in making good on that threat.

So what was Rafe doing down here?

Because when it came to Cathy Calderon, it seemed his brain could still get soft and a certain polar organ of his anatomy could still get hard and take over the brain-work. The same way it had the night when he'd seen her sparkly high heels fly over her wall, the same way it had when she'd hitched up her chiffon skirts and thrown her bare leg over the seat of his bike.

That improbable night had started off hot and had just gotten hotter.

He'd fallen hard and fast for Cathy Calderon. No other woman had ever gotten to him the way she had, and he'd thought she'd felt the same way about him.

As if it were yesterday, he remembered climbing on his motorcycle behind her, holding on to her waist and yelling the directions to his and Mike's house as they'd sped away through the warm dark night.

She'd been a natural on the big powerful bike.

A natural at other sports he'd liked even better.

If only he hadn't been dumb enough to think he could control the situation; dumb enough to forget that she was

Armi Calderon's stepdaughter. Dumb enough to forget that the rich always played mean and dirty.

With her chiffon skirts flying over his thighs, they'd raced along the 610 Loop past the Astrodome and then onto the empty Gulf Freeway, leaving her world behind and entering his.

"Where are we?" she whispered breathlessly when he'd told her to stop in front of a small clapboard house nestled under half a dozen tall pecan trees.

"Park Place," he muttered bitterly, seeing the peeling paint on all the bleak houses, the unmown yards, the burned-out house next door even in the darkness. "Pee Pee Town."

"Pee Pee Town?"

"Hey, nobody calls it that except me," he murmured with a guilty grin as he helped her off the bike and took her hand to lead her up the crumbling concrete driveway. "A lot of nice people still live out here, but it's damned sure not River Oaks."

"Count your blessings," she said almost wistfully. "At least you're free to come and go as you please."

"Right. 'Cause nobody gives a damn about me."

"Maybe that's not true anymore," she whispered a bit too possessively.

He caught her to him and for a moment stood there looking down at her. "You really think you're gonna stick around long enough to change things?"

"You'd better believe it."

He tried to make light of it. "I've been on my own since I was thirteen. Maybe I like things just like they are, Skinny. Maybe you're just a rich girl who's had every damn thing she's ever wanted, who thinks it'd be fun to go slumming."

She turned white. "No. Don't put yourself down like that. And the name's Cathy. Cathy Calderon."

He nodded and tried to look impressed, as if he didn't already know.

She smiled her cute smile. "And you don't like things the way they are. Any more than I do. My life's not so great, you know. What I want more than anything is to escape."

"Rafe Steele," he murmured, leaning down and fumbling in a flower bed till he dug up his front-door key. Then he unlocked the door and stood back, bowing slightly as if she were a princess, letting her enter first. "After you, Skinny."

"Cathy!"

"Right. Cathy," he drawled her name as he followed her inside.

When he saw her dark eyes taking in the green shag carpet that needed vacuuming and the rest of the awful mess Mike had made, Rafe quickly began peeling his roommate's clothes off the backs of the chairs and piano bench and dirty beige couch. There were a pair of lacy panties and nylons draped over the brass chandelier.

The mess was a good sign. Maybe it meant Mike was home.

Rafe grabbed the feminine lingerie and then knelt down and started picking up the newspapers and beer cans from the floor.

Standing up again, his arms dripping with a tangle of clothes and newspapers, Rafe said sheepishly, "I wasn't perfectly straight about... the hideout. I didn't tell you about my roommate. He gets sloppy when I'm not here to nag." Louder he yelled, "Yo—Mike! Company."

A chair was pushed back in the kitchen. Heavy footsteps resounded across a linoleum floor, then a swinging door that separated the bright yellow kitchen from the messily stacked dining room was pushed open.

"Yo—brother!" A dark, muscular figure in a white T-shirt and torn jeans leaned negligently against the doorjamb. "Long time no see!" rumbled a deep friendly voice. "I didn't expect you tonight. Manuel told me he sent you out on the Calderon job."

"Hey, this *is* Cathy Calderon. Cathy, meet Mike Washington," Rafe cut in pointedly, his intense blue gaze glaring warningly at Mike. He strutted around the corner and pitched all Mike's junk into his bedroom and slammed the door, which jammed on the pair of lacy panties.

"I like a man who knows that having fun is more important than keeping house," Cathy said with a giggle, picking up the panties and helpfully tossing them inside, too.

"Then I'm your man," Mike boomed, giving her a big white smile.

Mike was huge and black and as muscle-bound as a boxer. A thin scar ran the length of his right cheek.

"You're Cathy Calderon?" Mike was now frowning with deep disapproval.

"Mike," Cathy said ever so gently, going up to him, "lighten up. You don't have to worry. I know all about Rafe . . . and you and your little operation. He told me everything."

"*He did?*" Mike said, shooting Rafe a dark, startled look. "Manuel told me mum was the word on this job, brother."

"Things haven't changed—brother," Rafe said quietly.

"Then—"

"I was sneaking out of the house with a friend," Cathy continued.

"Her *friend* was drunk and tried to rape her," Rafe put in grimly.

"I don't think he would have gone that far, but when Rafe sweetly tried to rescue me, Jeff punched him out. I ended up saving Rafe."

Mike roared with laughter. "You're losing your touch."

"Do you have to tell him every damned detail, Skinny?"

"Am I missing something? I thought Mike was your partner... in crime. I was trying to reassure him."

"Crime? Say what?"

Rafe let out a long, exasperated sigh. "Cathy—do you have—"

"Let the lady talk, Rafe."

Rafe grabbed Cathy and pushed her toward the living room. "She's said too damned much already."

"So, how'd you figure out what Rafe was doing there?" Mike demanded. "Usually he plays it smarter than that."

"He told me."

"He what?"

Rafe strode past Cathy.

"Cathy, can I talk with the man here?" Rafe asked politely. "We need to have a private man-to-man chat."

"Sure," she said, smiling. "Don't mind me."

She stepped back and Rafe pushed Mike into the kitchen and then closed the door carefully.

Mike spun around. "What do you think you're doing?"

"Mike—hey, it's not like I planned this. I'm playing it by ear. And listen, she doesn't know I'm a bodyguard. I couldn't tell her that—'cause she hates bodyguards. The brat thinks I'm a thief."

"Say what?"

"She thinks you're one, too. But it's cool. She likes the idea."

"No, it's not cool, man. And you were stupid to bring her here."

"Yeah? Well, what was I supposed to do? Her father hired me to protect her. I couldn't leave her wandering around alone. No telling what she would have done next."

"So what are you planning to do? Spend the night with her—here?"

"Nothing I can't handle."

"Well, you'd better not *handle* Armi Calderon's daughter, if you get my drift. Or he'll handle you."

"Hey—I do have a three-digit IQ."

"But you're a low achiever."

"Not to worry. You're here to protect me."

Mike picked up his jacket. "Not for long."

"What?"

"Manuel put me on a job, too." Mike opened the back door and headed out. "One of Vadda Thomas's bodyguards walked out on her tonight after her concert."

Rafe whistled. Vadda was a beautiful soul singer. Mike was an avid fan. "At least she'll be more fun to look at than JoJo."

"My interest in her will be strictly professional, the way yours better be with Cathy Calderon. Don't cross the line—it always causes problems. Remember Consuelo—"

"Hey, I didn't—"

But Mike was gone.

And Rafe was alone with Cathy.

Which wouldn't have been so bad, because he'd taken Mike's advice to heart. Which wouldn't have been so bad since one of Rafe's credos was, Never, never sleep with a client.

Except that Cathy had ideas of her own.

Every time she smiled, it got harder and harder to remember that he had been hired to protect her, not ravish her; harder to remember that he was the pro, that he had the situation under control.

"Did Mike go out to steal?" she asked impishly.

Rafe nodded glumly.

Her face lit up. "Sounds like fun, but I'd rather stay here with you. How sweet of you to take the night off to entertain me."

"So—what do rich girls do for fun?"

"For starters, I want to watch you shave," she said, taking his hand and leading him to the bathroom. "Your whiskers made my skin burn. And I want to see what you really look like under there."

"And I thought it was my lips that made you hot."

"Your lips were okay," she said, smiling from the doorway, as he smeared lather on the lower part of his face and began to rake away a week's worth of black whiskers with the sure, deft strokes of Mike's razor. When Rafe was done, she came up to him, peering from behind him so she could see his face in the mirror.

"Better," she whispered in an awed tone as she studied his lean jaw and sensual mouth and rampantly male features. "Much better."

He spun around. "I was worried you wouldn't approve."

But she had already vanished into his bedroom. She came out a few minutes later wearing one of his shirts. Tangles of gold spilled messily out of her dangling diamond clips.

Damn those big liquid black eyes of hers, and that yellow hair. And why did her mouth have to look so succulent and moist?

He thought she looked incredibly sexy in his shirt. He wanted to kiss her, to taste her. To drag her into his bedroom for more.

"It's not too late for me to drive you home," he said hoarsely, reminding himself of his credo.

"Oh, no! I definitely want to stay here in the hideout with you."

"Right. And what do you want to do in the hideout?"

"Oh, anything," she whispered. "Everything." Her dark gaze was brilliant. "Maybe we could plan your next heist."

"Uh, how about some popcorn?"

While she wandered around the living room inspecting everything, he made popcorn. They watched an old movie together. Then they talked. Which was a mistake, because he found out he was right about the loneliness he had seen in her eyes.

She hadn't always been so rich. When she was eight, her mother, a moderately wealthy Houstonian, had married Armi Calderon, a Mexican national. Armi was a superwealthy, world-famous, international businessman in electronics and communications, real estate and mining. For a long time, Cathy had had a hard time believing all the houses and nannies located all over the world were for real. The only nanny who'd ever made her feel loved was someone named Pita who'd taken care of her in a remote Mexican village when the Calderons had been entertaining on their vast hacienda in Mexico.

Cathy told Rafe that her parents had jetted around the world, leaving her to be raised by paid employees. When her parents had shown up to see her, they always showered her with meaningless gifts they'd sent their servants out to buy. Armi had told her incessantly that no one would ever be as interested in *her* as much as in her money.

All his life, Rafe had thought of the rich being powerful, not vulnerable. He'd grown up with a sense of abandonment, and he'd never realized a rich child might have everything and still feel abandoned.

She explained that instead of making her happy, the Calderon money had made her feel trapped and vulnerable and isolated, less sure of herself, less sure of her friendships, less sure a man would ever want her just for herself.

Rafe had felt some hard part of himself softening for her as she described the way her family put money and power and status before everything else. The way they saw her as a pawn they expected to marry off to someone who was as rich as her stepfather. She was expected to make some brilliant economic alliance that would help diversify and enlarge two great fortunes.

Cathy told him of her real father, the man who her mother had married for love, the simple man who had retreated to his plantation to hunt and trap on the Louisiana bayous after her glamorous mother had divorced him to marry Armi so she could pursue her glittering social ambitions.

"My father died of a broken heart, but Mother doesn't care. Not because she's mean, but because she just doesn't understand what she did to him. All that matters to her are her beautiful houses and her beautiful friends and her beautiful parties. Everybody thinks she's so sweet. But the sweetness is not nearly the biggest part of her. My mother is every bit as ambitious and ruthless as Armi."

"I'm beginning to see why you climbed over that wall."

"I wasn't sneaking off with Jeff. I just needed someone to go for a walk in the gardens, somebody who was too scared of Armi to tell him I had run off after I ditched him."

"So where were you going tonight?"

"Anywhere—just away from them. I just needed space, freedom. I wanted to find a café, maybe talk to some real people. To be somewhere where I wasn't watched. I know that probably sounds silly to you."

When she lightly touched the back of his hand, the muscles of his forearm bunched. The heat emanating from her fingers felt good. Too good.

Rafe closed his eyes and took a deep tense breath and somehow managed to delude himself that he was still in control.

"I sure struck it lucky when I found you," she went on softly. Her shining eyes teased, luring him.

Rafe's throat tightened; he couldn't think of anything to say.

"But I don't want to talk about myself. I want to hear about you."

"There's not much to tell."

"Please . . ." Her voice trailed off.

He tried to tear his eyes away from her, but he couldn't. He was too aware of her warm compassionate nearness, of the sweetness of lavender, of her soft physical presence. She aroused all sorts of emotions so easily, emotions he could usually keep tightly controlled—the deep need for tenderness and for something as simple but essential as feminine friendship.

"Tell me," she whispered.

If he felt alarmed by the disturbing intimacy he felt toward her, he was stunned when he started spilling his guts. When he admitted he was the offspring of a fling his wealthy father had had with a Las Vegas show girl. When he told her about his unmarried mother blaming him for ruining her chances to be a big star. When he told her about his mother's drinking and boyfriends. And about Mike and him growing up in the same rough project and attending the same dangerous schools. About their becoming best friends in high school when they'd played football, about their learning to protect each other, and going to the University of Houston on football scholarships.

He thought maybe he was being a fool to reveal so much of himself, but her presence was curiously soothing.

"What did you major in?" she asked gently.

"Drama," he replied.

"Because you were talented?"

"Because I was lazy. Because lying came easy for me. I'd always had a knack for mimicking people's mannerisms, their accents. I used to want to be an actor. I even went out to Hollywood and got a few bit parts. I guess I took after my mother and wanted to be a star."

"Have you ever used any of it since then?"

He grinned. "All the time."

"I want to be a photographer when I get out of college."

She wanted to hear about why he and Mike had turned to crime after college, so he'd told her the tragic life story of a friend of a friend of his who hadn't been able to get a job after graduation and was now doing time in Huntsville. Rafe had learned a long time ago it was easier to use someone else's true story than to make up his own lie because it was easier to remember all the details later if he had to.

Rafe and she didn't do anything extraordinary, but just being with her began to feel extraordinary. She was barely more than a girl, but no other woman had ever touched so deep a chord within him.

Stifling a sleepy yawn, she slid across the couch and kissed him. Why he didn't jump up and run, he didn't know. He only knew he was powerless to do so.

What happened next had been inevitable from the first. There was only the briefest discussion.

"I've never had a rich girl before," he murmured as her lips nibbled his.

"I've never had a thief," she murmured softly.

"Then this will be a first for both of us."

"Yes." She drew a sharp little breath. "Are you going to talk all night?"

Her achingly sweet expression touched Rafe to the heart. "I was trying to be strong and noble."

"I thought maybe you didn't want me."

"Oh—I want you."

So much for control. So much for his lifelong credos. He was lost. And he knew it.

With a callused fingertip he traced the line of her nose. "But you're so young." His voice was husky. "Too young for me. And way too classy."

"What is this—honor among thieves?"

"Not exactly."

Cathy stared wordlessly at him as his finger moved from her nose to tilt her chin back. Then he bent his dark head to brush a soft, sweet kiss across her lips. Although his mouth lingered for less than a heartbeat, he felt an instant leaping excitement.

"I can't figure you out," she whispered against his mouth. "You were dressed like a thief, but then you tried to save me from Jeff. You've had me here practically all night in your hideout, and you haven't— I never thought a thief would be so protective, so gentlemanly."

Rafe's eyes warmed over her face as she reached up and unzipped his jacket.

Her glossy hair framed her delicate face like an aura. She was so beautiful, and somehow so vulnerable she stole the breath from his lungs. His pulse was throbbing as she stripped his jacket off. After a fumbling kiss or two, she shyly pulled his T-shirt over her head and tossed it behind him. Then she began to kiss him everywhere, with a shy urgency, as if all during the movie and their long conversation she had been waiting for this moment.

As he had. Even though he'd done everything in his power to prevent it.

Her lips paused when they came to his tattoo.

"What's the matter? Don't you go in for art?" he demanded huskily.

Still, she hesitated.

He twisted, and she gasped as he showed her the bandage in the center of his back. "That's where a—er, guard dog bit me last night."

She went white with shock.

"I haven't lived soft. Ready to run for cover, Skinny?"

"If only I could," she whispered almost desperately, caressing the hurt place very tenderly.

"I know the feeling."

He fused his mouth to hers. Very gently he lifted her in his arms and carried her to bed, getting up only to lock his bedroom door. When he came back to the bed, she reached for him and clung.

His eyes moved from the enchanting beauty of her face and tousled yellow hair down the creamy column of her throat. His expert fingers began to unbutton the shirt she'd borrowed from him. Slowly, almost reverently, he pushed the material aside and gently fondled her breasts, seeking her nipples.

She wrapped her legs around him and ran her hands down his spine. And the world began to spin faster and faster into the wild dark splendor of the night.

She flamed to his mouth and caresses as if she had been made for him. She did erotic things to him no other woman had ever done. At his every touch, she emitted soft purring sighs of pure sensation that made him know her blood pulsed as hotly as his. She was wild, wilder and more eager than any woman he'd ever had. Soon, even the lightest brushing of his lips across her heated flesh brought violent tremors of fresh desire shuddering through her.

When he slid his hand between her legs and she arched feverishly closer, he felt he would die if he didn't take her. Quickly, urgently, he lowered his body over hers and parted her thighs with his knee. But when he pushed inside, she cried out in startled anguish.

She was too tight, he realized in cold panic, recoiling instantly. With a frustrated groan, he rolled away from her glorious warmth to the far side of his bed, shocked to the core at the discovery that this wild eager girl was a virgin.

Of all the rotten luck...

"Don't you like me?" she whispered.

She was Armi Calderon's stepdaughter. He had heard unsavory rumors about what Calderon did to people who crossed him.

There were tears in her voice, and Rafe was as shaken as she was. He let a minute or two go by before he turned back and gently smoothed her hair. "Of course, I like you. I just don't like hurting you. I never would have done this . . . if I had thought for a second— Why didn't you tell me?"

"I acted like I was fast and experienced . . . because you looked like the kind of guy who was used to fast women. I was afraid you'd lose interest if I didn't."

"Oh, my God—"

She was very still. He could feel her staring up into the darkness. "How old were you the first time?" she asked.

"Fourteen," he replied thickly, not liking her question.

"There—you see?"

"That's got nothing to do with tonight!" He reached in a drawer for his cigarettes and shook one out. When it was lit, he inhaled deeply, slowly. "You and me—we're not alike. You've got to understand that—I grew up in a jungle."

"So did I."

"I should have *protected* you. I should never have touched you." His grim voice was filled with self-loathing. "I'm through with your bright ideas. I'm taking you home."

"I thought guys liked to be the first."

He squashed out his cigarette furiously. "For a virgin, you've got a lot of dumb ideas on this subject."

He was getting up angrily, when she reached for him, sliding her hand over his hair-roughened chest. "I don't care about being your first. All I care about is being your last."

"That's the stupidest thing you've said yet! Look— you and I come from two different worlds. I should never have let myself forget that. I'm a good ten years older than you. I don't have a dime. Nothing I could give you. It wouldn't work."

"I'm not going home."

"Okay." His voice was clipped. He grabbed a pillow and a blanket off the end of the bed. "But I'm sleeping on the couch."

That unsatisfactory arrangement lasted an hour.

Until he heard her cry, and the thin tragic sob tore through him like a knife.

He got up and went to her. For a long moment, he stood in the doorway, studying her, thinking he was weak not to be able to resist her tears. But he had caused them.

She lay in his bed, her loose, butter yellow hair spilling everywhere, her face buried in his pillow, her slender body shaking with sobs.

No matter what he did, he would hurt her. But he couldn't bear her thinking he wanted to reject her. So even though he knew he shouldn't, he went to her and with shaking hands pulled her into his hard arms, caressing and comforting her until she quieted.

Taking her sweet face gently between his hands, he tenderly kissed away her salty tears, murmuring apologies.

She leaned up toward him shyly and touched his cheek. "You've got to finish what you started."

"No!"

"Love me, Rafe. Please, just love me. I—I can't begin to tell you how much I need you. You say we come from different worlds, but I don't fit in with my family's world. I never will. I know you're a thief and I'm a millionaire's stepdaughter, so I'm not asking for tomorrow. Just for tonight. All my life...I've been so alone. Please, Rafe ... I just want to be with you."

He understood the desperate pain in her voice because he'd lived with the same kind of loneliness. He'd prided himself on being tough and independent. In the past he'd used women for sex and steered clear of real closeness. Somehow he knew that wasn't going to be possible with her.

In a flash of blinding insight, she stripped him of his protective shell. He had to have her. Even though he already knew he wanted way more than her body. Even though he already sensed they were doomed.

Very gently he kissed her mouth. Within seconds they were both on fire, and his hands were in her tangled hair, fiercely pulling her toward him. Soon he was lost to the tantalizing pleasure of her burning mouth and delectable body melting into his.

When he flipped her onto her back and eased himself into her, this time pushing very very gently, she kissed him bravely, with only the tiniest moan escaping her lips. After the first tight stroke, she relaxed and, smiling radiantly up at him, opened herself to him endlessly, and he took everything she had to offer because he was even more starved for it than she.

The final rapture was soul-shattering; the joy he found in her was so wondrously profound it seemed boundless. He made love to her a second time and a third, and each time it was better. Each time made him know that he wanted more than tonight. More than tomorrow.

He was staking a claim on forever.

He had found a tenderness in loving her that his life, for all its adventure and physical passion, had lacked until this one night with her.

But later, as Rafe lay awake in the first glowing light of dawn, his hard body moist and cool with sweat as he cuddled her close, he was coldly furious with himself.

Out of all the virgins in the world to bed, he could hardly have made a more dangerous choice than Armi Calderon's stepdaughter.

Sooner or later, Calderon was bound to find out.

And when he did, there would be hell to pay.

Four

In spite of his black cowboy hat, the sun was in Rafe's eyes as he drove. And no matter how he positioned himself on the seat cover of his truck, he couldn't get comfortable. Which was partly because he was sitting on the 9-mm Browning automatic pistol and a pair of handcuffs he'd hidden under the cover. And partly because the traffic was heavy and dangerously fast. Like too many roads in Mexico, this twisting, rubble-strewn rut with no shoulders somewhere in the Sierra Madre Occidentals was under construction.

Hell—the poor bastards on the sides of the road were practically building it by hand. He'd had to swerve no less than a dozen times to keep from hitting the laborers with picks and shovels who were chopping and hacking like slaves. An even greater hazard was the numerous street vendors clogging the shoulders selling huaraches, leather purses, belts and fruit drinks.

Suddenly, an overly zealous vendor leaped onto Rafe's running board and mashed a dead-looking iguana up against the glass. The paralyzed creature looked both pitiful and frightful—like a lot of the animals down here. Like a lot of the people. Like he'd look himself, if Armi Calderon tipped off the wrong people that he was here. Rafe shook his head and slowed the truck, so the nut could jump off and try the next vehicle.

Damn! This country! These people.

But what he damned most of all was a beautiful girl with great dark Spanish eyes and glorious masses of golden hair that never did what it was supposed to do. Her hair clips came loose; her sophisticated knots unraveled at her slender nape, and tendrils of the silken stuff flew everywhere.

Six and a half years ago, he'd had a yen for butter yellow hair and vulnerable dark eyes. A yen for the high-spirited rich girl who didn't know how to dress and couldn't fit into her family's glitzy world.

More than a yen.

No longer.

She'd taken his heart and his soul.

Armi Calderon had taken everything else.

The road veered west. Rafe pulled down the visor, and dust poured swirling into his lap. Long clouds of the powdery stuff were spewing out from behind the pickup's rear wheels and out from behind every other vehicle's as well.

It was almost impossible to see, so he slowed his pickup when he took the blind curve. It was almost too late when he heard the blaring horn. Suddenly, a bus whose brakes had failed, barreled out of the powdery plumes straight at him like a roller-coaster car flying off its track.

All he could see was chrome and steel.

He was going to die!

Rafe yanked the wheel hard to the right. With a shudder, he felt the bus crush his door into his elbow as it sideswiped him. The pickup jerked, careened, scraping against the jagged limestone mountain on his right side, as well. Mirrors and door handles crumpled and tore off.

Then the bus was behind him, lost somewhere in the boiling dust, and Rafe's truck shuddered violently against a big boulder and came to a standstill.

Rafe's seat belt caught at the very last moment. His air bag exploded. He hit his head on something, anyway, which bloodied the right side of his forehead. Other than the cut and a few scratches on his face from the air bag, he was okay. But one look at his truck after he kicked out the window, and he knew it was totaled.

An hour later, the traffic jam was at least a half a mile long on either side of the accident.

There was a huge crowd of lean, dark men holding ropes and shovels and crowbars gawking and discussing the dilapidated bus with its back tire hanging off the cliff. And every time another car or truck was forced to stop, one more driver would get out, grab a tool or anything he thought might be useful and march up the crumbling road to the wreck to talk to the bus driver to see what could be done. Rural Mexicans hadn't formed the gringos' habit of waiting for law officials to solve their problems.

The dust had settled, and the empty bus now sat at a faint tilt, looking as dead and lost as a beached whale, its third-class carcass almost entirely, but not quite, blocking the road. A forlorn plastic crucifix dangled from the rearview mirror. A bald back tire hung over a nothingness that fell thousands of feet to a river that boiled away into a lost chasm.

A neatly folded, snapped denim shirt and Rafe's black Stetson with its jaunty peacock feather lay on a large rock beside the bus. There was a peaceful quality about these items that belied the savage impatience their owner had felt as he'd slowly stripped out of them and gently laid them out of harm's way.

Rafe needed to get in and out of this country—fast. Before the wrong people traced the plates on his truck and found out for sure he was here.

The laborers had quietly convinced him that the thing to do was to attach two ropes to the front axle of the bus so they could pull it back on the road.

Primitive solution—but hell, it just might work in Mexico.

Rafe was now halfway under the bus with only the pointed tips of his scuffed brown boots sticking out. His usually glossy black head was caked with dirt as he tugged furiously against the second hemp rope he'd tied around the axle. When it broke, he fell hard into a nasty puddle of grease and rocks, cutting his wide bare shoulders. He let out a great rumble of profanity. At the same time, he kicked out in frustration at whatever had begun pecking curiously at the cuffs of his jeans.

His boot heel raised a cloud of dust as he sent the squawking rooster flying straight toward Jesús, the macho bus driver, and the clump of Mexican laborers clustered under the scrawny jacaranda tree clinging to the cliff. The tree was the single source of shade against the harsh sun.

Impatient as Rafe was that this ordeal was taking way too long—any minute the cops might show up—his cynical mouth curved with dark humor at the sight of a dozen dirty brown feet in worn huaraches scampering in terror from the enraged rooster.

He twisted his dark head and bronzed torso out from under the bus and held up the frayed ends of the rope and shouted, *"No es bueno!"* No good! As always, the flat drawl that made him sound ridiculous even in English anywhere off his ranch in the Texas hill country brought smirks.

A small grinning boy rushed up to him with a stouter-looking length of hemp.

"Nuevo, señor," the boy said proudly. *"Fuerte."* New and strong.

"Gracias," Rafe grumbled, edging his long lean body back under the bus. A blisteringly hot, black drop oozed from the bus and scalded his belly. He jumped, yelping like he'd been branded as he banged his forehead again.

The bloody place above his eyebrow began to throb. As he wrapped the hemp around the axle, he was sure that hell was dust and flies and anything to do with Spanish. Hell was All Saints' Day or All Souls' Day—or whatever you called this two-day farce that had every Mexican jamming the highways. Hell was coming back to a country where there was a price on his head and getting anywhere near Cathy and Armi Calderon.

Rafe jerked hard against the new rope.

It held.

As he inched himself out from under the bus, he couldn't avoid all the rocks or pools of grease. Normally he would have let one of the laborers do a job this dirty, but this was *mañana* land, and he wanted to get the show on the road.

The ragged Indian boy who'd brought the rope squatted, his wide smile shy and friendly. The boy began jerking a string so that the legs of his paper skeleton flapped.

Rafe smiled gently back at him and then glanced beyond him to the leather-faced Mexican farm workers in their straw cowboy hats, canvas pants and worn huaraches who had regrouped under the jacaranda tree. They were smoking and drinking sodas. Every time they looked over the vertical drop to the narrow river, they crossed and recrossed themselves. Rafe listened as each farmer excitedly repeated his version of the burning smell right before the bus had slewed around that final curve.

Suddenly, from the road behind the boy and the men, two short, impatient toots rang out in perfect rhythm with the movements of the kid's puppet.

Incredible as it seemed, a small car was boldly making its way through the stopped cars.

Rafe swiveled on his shoulders in the dirt and saw the bottom edge of a red fender and a shiny chrome bumper gliding toward him. If he didn't stay under the bus, the idiot would run over his legs.

Rafe's head was too far under the bus to tell what kind of car it was, other than it was a sports car.

"Güera!" The laborers hooted.

There was obviously a beautiful woman in the car.

Suddenly, Rafe's blue eyes narrowed on the radial tire inching toward his—

"Not my hat!"

Scrunch.

Yes, his hat.

He saw the huge black marks across denim; then, the crushed row of snaps down the front of his shirt.

"Damn!"

With a lunge, Rafe hurled himself out from under the bus to give the thoughtless driver a piece of his mind.

Then he saw *her.*

Or rather the back of masses of butter gold flyaway hair. She waved gaily at each driver and then at the laborers, who were now clapping and shouting, "Bravo!"

Only one woman had messy hair like that—part flame, all sunlight and perfumed silk.

Rafe went hot, then cold.

Cathy—

She hadn't changed.

Or if she had, she was more beautiful than ever.

Rafe ducked back under the bumper. He'd taken a Peruvian freedom fighter's bullet in his shoulder that had been meant for Consuelo. He'd been stabbed when he'd gone into an African prison to free an executive held hostage. He'd been bitten in the back by a groupie. Armi's thugs had kicked in seven of his ribs. More recently, he'd been pinned down for seventeen hours by terrorists' firepower in Angola, where he'd gone on a routine job for the U.S. Government to act as a collections specialist and verify some rather disturbing satellite information about the country's military movements.

Rafe's business was do or die.

But the last thing he needed was for Cathy to see him now and tell the wrong people, or he'd end up dead in some deep ravine with a bullet in his back.

If he got lucky, maybe he'd be in Texas tomorrow, and he'd never have to set eyes on her again.

But the sight of Cathy's pale, slender fingers resting on that leather steering wheel brought a rush of unwanted memories that made his mouth go dry. He remembered those innocent hands running over his body, doing talented things a man like him could never forget.

His heart began to pound.

For a few brief months they'd had so damned much fun.

He'd fallen madly in love the first night he met her.

Things had gone great till he'd gone for the guy who'd pointed a gun at Armi's heart, and Cathy had found out Rafe was really her bodyguard.

Then she had refused to listen to anything he said. He'd figured out it was really a class thing. She'd liked sneaking around with a thief. But the last thing she wanted was an open, honest relationship with someone she considered a low-class boytoy. She'd thought she was better than him—the same way his father had thought himself better than his mother.

When Rafe had gone down on his knees and begged her to marry him, thinking to rescue her from a life she had told him she hated, she'd shouted furiously, "What kind of fool do you take me for? I hate you! You are the last, the very last man I would ever marry!"

Almost his father's words.

Then she'd used her money to erect an impregnable barrier. She'd told Armi to pay him off, to pay him a fortune because he was so multitalented he'd earned every penny.

His own father had left a suitcase full of money.

Then she'd boarded Armi's private jet and flown with her mother to the Italian Riviera. For the next month, there had been write-ups about Cathy and a dozen titled boyfriends. Then suddenly, she had fled Europe and vanished. Curiously, Rafe had missed the sensational stories even though they'd brought pain, for not knowing about her was even worse. Except for a few articles in financial magazines about Armi's lavish life-style and dangerously aggressive tactics in highly leveraged takeovers that had brought governmental investigators down on him, there hadn't been anything on Cathy till she'd started dating Maurice Dumont.

Rafe had written her, but his letters had come back. He had found out too late that Cathy had been the biggest mistake in his life, because she'd made him feel abandoned and all alone the way he had when his father had walked out. Then Rafe had found out too late what a man like Armi Calderon did to a man he believed had double-crossed him. Together, Armi and Cathy had put Rafe through hell and damn near destroyed him.

After Cathy, Rafe had been so emotionally bankrupt, he'd felt more dead than alive. The few times he'd used women for sex, he'd felt only emptier and lonelier. The only thing that made him know he was still alive was the thrill he got out of his dangerous missions.

He had felt alive when he'd seen the picture of the pixie-faced imp Manuel had claimed was Rafe's.

"Cathy..."

When Rafe mouthed her name in toneless rage, the yellow dust swirled up from the road, choking him.

The top of her car was down, and her long fire gold curls shimmered in the sun as they blew around her delicate nape. He knew just how soft her hair was, how it smelled like sunshine and lavender after she washed it and climbed into bed with him, her body still damp and cool from the shower but growing hot almost as soon as he'd stroked her.

Her bare arms and shoulders were flushed from too much sun. Didn't she know fair skin couldn't take the sun?

Hell—Cathy never did what she was supposed to.

He remembered those arms wrapped around his naked body when she had clung to him. God, she'd been wild in bed. And sweet and funny out of it. God, how hard he'd worked to forget the happy times.

But he hadn't forgotten a single hour. He remembered the night he'd serenaded her and told her he loved her.

His thundering heart doubled its beat. He forced himself to remember that he hated her. That the last thing he needed was to involve himself with Cathy again. That the last thing he needed was more of Calderon's people bringing more of their false wire-tapping charges against him. Rafe was still deeply in debt from all the legal battles from fighting Armi's people in court.

Cathy Calderon and her nut case of a stepfather were bad news.

Suddenly, Cathy's bright head turned toward the elegant blond man beside her in her car whose hand possessively stole up her arm. With a raw jolt of anger, Rafe looked away, unable to watch the rich jerk paw her.

So, that was the much-written-about blue blood she was to marry—Maurice Dumont, the damned French aristocrat whose father owned bunches of castles.

The glittering couple in the bright red sports car looked so damned rich, so self-important—so spoiled. So happy and carefree—like they believed they could buy anybody or anything they wanted. So perfect for each other.

So perfect that it was impossible to imagine Cathy had an illegitimate, pixie-faced daughter hidden away in a poverty-stricken Mexican village.

Manuel had to be out of his mind.

Or did he?

Cathy Calderon had never played by the rules.

Professional concerns came swiftly to Rafe. A rich beautiful woman had no business on a road like this where anybody who wanted her could take her and hold her for ransom.

Maybe she was crazy, but if that titled jerk really loved her, he wouldn't let her drive around Mexico in a showy car without her bodyguards when he clearly wasn't man enough to protect her.

And Cathy, who had grown up with bodyguards, had to know the risk she was taking.

Rafe swallowed against the sinking sensation in the pit of his stomach. Not that she cared about risks. *But why was she here?*

Why was she sneaking off with Maurice to the same remote Mexican village Rafe was on his way to? Why weren't she and her fancy boyfriend down in the valley at Armi's hacienda enjoying their wedding guests?

Had she told Maurice she had a blue-eyed little girl? Was Cathy planning for him to adopt her?

Two more toots of the horn, and the red car made it past the bus and his truck. The laborers cheered as Cathy got out and took several pictures of the bus and the truck before driving away.

When he was sure Cathy was gone, Rafe scrambled out from under the bus. Two dozen Mexicans grabbed the shabby ropes trailing from under the bumper. A peasant woman in an embroidered cotton blouse walked up to him hawking marigolds.

Rafe shook his head and, pulling his wallet from his back pocket, flipped it open to the snapshot.

Damn. The pixie-faced creature had the bluest eyes! Just like his mother's! *Just like his own!*

What the hell was he going to do if the kid was for real?

Slowly, Rafe bent down and picked up the dust-covered, broken felt pancake that had once been his hat. He slapped it against his thigh to shake the dust out of it. He ripped out the frazzled feather and then punched at the brim, reshaping the thing as best he could before carefully setting it on his dark head.

He had the oddest sinking feeling that he was in way too deep.

Maybe he should just walk away.

The way Cathy had.

The way his father had.

But Rafe wasn't like them.

He had to know.

And if the kid was his, he'd claim her.

No matter what it cost him.

Five

Either he'd gotten a bad attitude after the grinning mechanic told him his truck was totaled, or this barren mountain village really was uglier than most Rafe had seen this far south of the border. There were no trees, nothing green. His entire impression would have been of dust, skinny dogs, barefoot kids, junked cars, ramshackle sidewalks and rutted roads had the streets not been strewn with marigolds and the village noisily alive with an infectious gaiety.

Rafe tried to ignore the bizarre sensation that magic was in the air as he strode swiftly up the crowded, cobblestoned street, counting the huts because there were no street signs.

Men were jammed into doorways, drinking tequila and talking. They eyed him curiously. All he noted about them was that they weren't drinking the good kind of tequila.

He passed a baker's shop with grinning skeletons painted onto the windows. He was tired of traveling, sick of the delays, furious about his truck, hungrier than hell, but ready to get where he was going and find out what he wanted to know—and then hightail it back to Texas.

Finally, when he climbed higher, the madness and the crowds and the houses thinned out.

A dark boy rushed toward him out of the purple blackness. "Eh, gringo. Chicles?"

The little tough was appealing, but he had the look of a lot of kids down here. He had old eyes in a young face.

Rafe peeled a dollar out of his wallet, but when he held it out to the kid, the kid took one look at him and gasped. Black eyes popped from beneath thick inky bangs; his dark face turned sickly gray. When Rafe leaned down to give him the dollar, the kid screamed in mortal terror. Gum exploded everywhere. Then the kid bolted.

Rafe knew he had to look a sight. Half the broken snaps on his shirt were undone, and a thin coating of chalklike dust covered every inch of his tall body—from the whitened brim of his battered black hat to the pointed toes of his boots. There was a rip in his black leather jacket, and he didn't smell too pleasant. But Mexican street toughs didn't scare easily, even young ones, and there was no way the kid could have spotted the 9-mm Browning automatic jammed in the back of Rafe's waistband.

Rafe was perplexed. First time down here he'd ever seen a kid selling Chicles run from an American dollar.

Rafe forgot the kid and kept climbing until he counted the twentieth house. There he turned onto a much narrower, darker, dead-end street. Fifty meters farther and his chest tightened when he saw the white walls and the red-roofed house—exactly as Manuel had described them. There was a single guard washing a red sports car in front of the massive Spanish doors cut into the white wall.

Getting inside would be a piece of cake. But the dead-end street made him nervous. He didn't like places with only one way in and one way out. Swiftly, Rafe cut around the back, scrambling up a steep cliff behind the house. When he saw the darkened holes in the mountain face, he realized they must be the ruined mine shafts Manuel had told him about.

Knowing he could be shot for climbing a wall in Mexico, Rafe jumped onto Cathy's, anyway.

A cute white playhouse that was a replica of the larger white mansion dominated the courtyard.

Somebody had a kid, all right.

Rafe paused, drawing a jerky breath.

Relax. A dumb playhouse doesn't have to mean you're a father.

Just as Rafe was about to swing himself over, he saw the same little Indian tough who'd dropped his chicles crawling over the opposite wall. The boy sprang onto the patio as lithely as a cat. Rafe let himself down, too, racing after him, keeping to the shadows.

When the kid reached the house, he tossed a rock up to a second-story window and called out a name. "Sadie!"

Sadie. It was just a name, but it singed Rafe like electricity.

The upstairs window flew open.

And a tiny figure with long golden hair and a tall pointy hat stuck her head out excitedly. The tall hat bobbed up and down. Furtively, she put her fingers to her lips and pointed to the room next to hers. Then she vanished, only to reappear in the next microsecond at the door of the balcony.

The brat moved like lightning.

Rafe saw that the tall pointy hat matched her trailing black gown. He felt vaguely uneasy as he remembered how he'd loved costumes as a kid. Uneasier still as he thought of the charge he still got when he worked undercover.

Even as he reassured himself their mutual liking for disguises didn't have to mean anything, he felt a pulse begin to throb where he'd bumped his forehead.

Was this miniature, hyperactive brat his daughter?

No daughter of *his* would sneak out at the age of six to meet a street kid.

Then why did he feel this strange mixture of complex, unwanted, paternal emotions as he watched her lean down, struggle impatiently with her long skirt and unbuckle her shoes? Slipping them into her pockets, she stealthily tiptoed across the balcony.

"What do you want, Juanito?" she whispered, sounding excited and yet annoyed, too, in flawless Spanish.

If she was his daughter, she'd better speak English, too. *If she was his daughter... Get real!*

As Rafe inched closer, a twig broke under his heel.

Both kids jumped as if they'd heard a bullet.

"What was that, Juanito?"

"A ghost, maybe. They're out, you know."

In big-eyed silence they searched the shadows and trees.

"I don't see anything," Sadie said in a scared whisper.

The little thug's chest swelled with self-importance. "Well, I saw one already."

"I don't believe you, Juanito!"

"I saw your father!"

Rafe went as still as death.

He wanted to spring out and scream it wasn't true, but he was too petrified to move.

"When?" Sadie bobbed up and down on the tips of her toes. "Where?"

"A few minutes ago. In the street. I tried to sell him some chicles."

"Ghosts don't buy chicles, stupid!"

Ghosts? What was that supposed to mean?

"He just took 'em."

"Now I know you're lying, Juanito."

She had that right.

"No! He had a cowboy hat just like the one in your mother's picture, but he's cut his ponytail. And he was all dirty and scratched and spooky-looking just like he'd crawled out of his grave! And he smelled like he was about half-rotten, too!"

"Wow!"

"Come down! And I'll show you where I saw him!"

The miniature witch looked over the railing. With an imperious flick of her wrist, she sent her pointy hat sailing down to him. When he caught it and put it on his own black head, she giggled. Carefully gathering her long skirts in one arm, she jumped up onto the balcony railing and grabbed a branch of the tree beside the house.

"Why don't you just take the stairs?" Juanito asked.

"'Cause Mommy's in her room and she might see me!"

Sadie glanced down again and lost her balance. As her arms waved wildly and she teetered, Rafe felt paralyzed by a sheer, gutless terror until she steadied herself. Rafe held his breath as the imp, with the ease and grace of a gibbon monkey, swung herself down along the branch hand over hand till she reached the trunk. There was another scary moment when her dress ripped on a twig and she almost fell again.

Then she jumped down, and Juanito took her hand. The look of intense excitement and great affection that passed between them reminded Rafe of his own childhood friendship with Mike. Then they raced to the wall where Juanito had come from, and scaling it, they slipped over it, vanishing into the darkness together.

Obviously this was no new trick.

Obviously Cathy had absolutely no control over Sadie.

Cathy had never been into control.

If she hadn't been the free-spirited product of too much control, she would never have fallen for him.

The question was—was the miniature blond witch his daughter?

He hoped fervently that she was not.

But there was only one way to find out.

The tall brilliantly lit windows with the flowing gauzy curtains, and the unlocked doors of Cathy's house made surveillance as easy as taking candy from a baby, so easy he wouldn't need the glasses he used for night vision. Rafe crept along the balcony in the dark, peering into every window and trying every door to see which was locked and which wasn't.

He even sneaked inside, into the empty living room, where he studied the photographs of Cathy and the school she had started in the village, of Cathy and the shelter and soup kitchen she had built for the village poor. There were stacks of photograph albums filled with pictures of Sadie as a baby, as a toddler. There were pictures of a laughing Cathy doing things with her daughter; of Cathy doing good works and surrounded by appreciative poor villagers. In one picture, Sadie and Juanito were hanging upside down like possums from trapezes. In another, Sadie was squirting Juanito in the face with a yard sprinkler.

Rafe remembered Cathy saying that she had started taking pictures as a child because her parents never took any pictures of their family. The only photographs had been of the glittering couple with celebrities and royalty.

Rafe remembered that Cathy had said she dreamed of having a normal life. She had wanted to fill photograph albums with pictures of her children and husband and pets and genuine friends. She had taken dozens of rolls of him. Rafe wished he had more time for the albums, but when he heard a sound, he stepped quickly back out onto the balcony.

Thirty minutes later he had the layout.

He had a lot more than a layout. He had a plan.

From the shadows, he had watched Maurice try to make love to Cathy when they had come out onto the terrace. The awkward little scene had been short and sweet, Cathy begging that they save the hot stuff for the bedroom because she was utterly terrified Sadie might be spying and pop out of the woodwork at just the wrong moment.

Terrified. That had been her exact word.

From the snatches he could catch of their rather heated conversation that had to do with another kiss and a suitcase full of iguanas, Rafe had concluded that the miniature witch was not exactly pleased with the snooty French aristocrat Cathy planned to marry.

From the shadows, Rafe had watched Pita cooking in the kitchen. He had seen her uncork a bottle of champagne and set it in an ice bucket. When she had leaned over it and shaken a vial of pink powder down its long neck just as if she were salting the cavity of a chicken, he would have given anything to break cover and go inside and ask her what the hell she was up to. But the scene got stranger. Like a kid reciting a difficult poem she'd memorized for class, Pita had picked up an old book and read from it aloud to a large framed photograph of a stern-looking Indian woman.

As Pita read, Rafe got cold all over, the way one did when a Texas norther blew in. Only there wasn't a norther. It was something weird and spooky. Then the blue flames under the teakettle on the gas burner turned green, and the golden frame of the photograph reflected the same eerie color.

Pita closed her book, and, with a satisfied smile, patted the bottle of champagne and laid the photograph down beside it. Then Rafe remembered he had to go, because Cathy and Maurice were already upstairs.

So, he'd crept up to the second-story balcony and observed Maurice undressing. Cathy, too. Only he had watched Cathy longer.

When she came out of her bathroom wearing only a towel with her yellow hair spilling everywhere, he couldn't move. Then she let the towel drop, and his blood ran like fire in his veins. For a long moment, she stood at the mirror, eyeing herself critically.

Then she began to do things. First she slathered lotion all over her body. Hungrily, he watched her fingers sliding everywhere, lingering on her breasts, her stomach and thighs. When she was done, he thought that would be the end of it.

But no, she brought her hands under her delectable breasts and lifted them higher, inspecting the luscious lobes, the perky nipples. Then she paraded in front of her mirror, striking seductive poses. She stood on her tiptoes and stuck one of her long gorgeous legs up on the counter. She arched her spine, played with her hair, holding it up and then letting it fall all over her shoulders in thick glorious tangles.

Rafe groaned hoarsely as jealous rage and desire shuddered through him. Was she practicing those teasing love games because she intended to use them on Maurice?

When Rafe remembered how she'd played fast and easy with him that first night when she'd been trying so hard to impress a bad-boy thief, he had to clench his hands to keep from going in and grabbing her and giving her what she so obviously wanted. Maybe if he hadn't had her before, he wouldn't feel this sudden hot possessive fury that she was his and no other man should ever touch her. Or maybe if he didn't know just how great she was in bed, he wouldn't have found her lush body and wanton strutting so damned appealing.

But as usual, she'd pushed him over some fatal edge and reduced him to an animal. By the time she pulled on her transparent black nightgown, his brain had shorted out from overload, and that rebel polar organ lodged in his too-tight, dirty jeans that never thought straight had begun to harden and burn with a lot of dumb ideas of its own.

That's when the plan had hit him.

It would mean crossing the line.

She'd had that effect on him before.

His lips curved in a bitter smile, and he yanked his 9-mm Browning out of his waistband. Emptying the bullets into the palm of his shaking hand, he counted them twice, one by one, just to make sure he had them all.

Then he stuffed them into his back pocket along with the handcuffs. He needed the gun for scaring, not for killing.

The unsuspecting Maurice was still singing in the shower when Rafe came up behind him and jammed the muzzle into the small of his spine.

Never before had Rafe deliberately terrorized an innocent man.

There wasn't a scuffle. Just a brief, whispered, no-nonsense conversation. Not so brief that Rafe didn't have time to note the cultured French accent. Not so brief that the hatefully smug, white-faced aristocrat couldn't angrily select a few items from his wardrobe that would be perfect for Rafe's masquerade in the little seduction scene he intended to play for Cathy. Not so brief that he didn't apologize to the naked Maurice as he quickly handcuffed and gagged him. Binding his ankles together, Rafe locked him in his closet with a couple of blankets and a pillow.

Rafe showered and shaved and dabbed on some of Maurice's fancy French after-shave. Then he dressed in black slacks and a black silk turtleneck and a gray cashmere blazer. The black suede shoes were a little tight, but the rest was okay.

As he ran Maurice's comb through his short dark hair, Rafe thought of Cathy's dark nipples peeping through the black lace.

This was better than okay. Better than his usual undercover stuff.

The silk was smooth and soft against his skin.

Very nice.

But playing around with Cathy was going to be nicer.

Six

Cathy whirled at the feather-light knock at her bedroom door, spilling the glass of champagne she was holding all over her hand and black filmy peignoir. She was so nervous, she just gulped down what was left in the goblet, and, taking the bottle out of the ice bucket, poured herself another glass. Then she poured one for Maurice.

Not that she believed for one minute that Pita's love potion would work. It was just that she needed the champagne to get through the awkwardness of tonight.

Odd, how the thought of making love had never, not even the first time, seemed awkward with Rafe.

But Rafe had been so earthy and wild, he'd made her feel the same way. Maurice was a much more refined breed—a much superior breed, she hastily reassured herself.

Maurice's second knock was softer than the first. But to Cathy it thudded deadlier. In spite of her bubble bath and all the lotions and perfume she'd doused herself with to make herself feel sexy, in spite of her clingy black lace gown and filmy peignoir, she felt about as much enthusiasm for the project ahead as if she were condemned to die and about to face her executioner.

Hastily, she choked down a second glass, nearly strangling on the frothy bubbles.

"Come in...darling." Her attempted purr that was supposed to sound alluringly sophisticated sounded shaky and unsure. "I left the door open...darling." Oh, why did that endearment stick like a dry, dead lump in her mouth?

The door cracked and she saw Maurice's elegant, black-sleeved hand reach in and turn off the light.

Oh, why hadn't she thought of that? Maurice was so very elegant and refined, so exquisitely considerate to understand that things would be so much easier for her in the dark.

And it was very dark, because she'd locked the balcony doors and drawn the second heavier curtains behind the sheers.

"Where are you, my darling?" he asked.

Maybe it was the champagne, but Maurice's low, French-accented voice sounded huskier than usual. A wanton, electric thrill coursed through her. Maybe this wasn't going to be so bad, after all. Or was there really something in that love potion Pita had been so silly with excitement about?

No—that was too ridiculous to even consider.

"I'm over here," Cathy answered less nervously.

He zeroed in on her like a nocturnal hunter, as swift and surefooted as a panther in the velvet darkness. His broad-shouldered body loomed expectantly over her.

Maurice had never seemed quite so tall, or her room so small. She, too, felt tinier beside him. When the next thrilling tingle traced the length of her spine, she really did begin to believe a little in magic.

She handed him a glass, and when their fingers brushed, his felt harder, more callused than Maurice's— hotter, too. She drew back jerkily at the unexpected shock of his warmth.

When he jumped back, as well, a new primal tension seemed to leap between them. Shrugging his shoulders, Maurice was the first to recover.

She saw the faintest flicker of moonlight on crystal as he lifted his glass. Strange, how the gesture seemed almost defiant.

His aim was unerring in the dark; his handcut goblet clinked against hers.

"To us," she whispered throatily.

"Ditto." He bit out the word.

Ditto? Where had that come from? Usually, Maurice's faintly accented English was so cultured.

Maurice speedily drained his glass. Usually, he took his time over food or wine or good champagne.

Odd, how he suddenly reminded her of a certain other, much rougher, lower-class individual with far lustier appetites.

She attributed the odd behavior to Maurice's excitement. To her nerves.

For no reason at all, she thought of Pita's glowing black eyes when the woman had brought her the potion-laced bottle of champagne.

Dear God.

The spell was supposed to make her fall in love with Maurice, not fantasize about Rafe.

Cathy set her glass down abruptly, for already she felt an incredible heat bubbling through her arteries.

"Don't you want your champagne?" he murmured.

"I—I feel so hot."

"So do I." He put his glass down beside hers, so that the edge of its bottom was balanced precariously on top of hers. "That's how we're supposed to feel," came his disturbingly low tone.

When he moved closer, she nearly jumped out of her skin.

"Easy," he whispered gently, soothingly.

"It's just that it's been so long," she murmured.

"How...long?"

Neither of them noticed that his French accent had altered slightly.

"Six and a half years," she whispered. Just thinking about Rafe made her feel weak.

For a moment, he stood without moving in that silent darkness.

"Who was he?" Maurice demanded tightly, his tension almost explosive.

After a long time, she replied in a low, choking tone. "Sadie's father, of course! I've told you before there's never been anyone but him."

She heard him catch his breath as if he'd suffered some great shock, and the quick rasp of that harsh sound was deeply unsettling. When he reached savagely for his glass of champagne, it tipped and shattered. "Sorry," he muttered.

"It doesn't matter."

He gulped from her glass and then poured himself another.

Pita had said the more he drank, the more powerful the effect would be.

Which was utter nonsense.

"Maurice, there is no reason for you to be upset. It's been over for six long years."

"You're sure?" His tone was lower, rougher—different.

"Quite . . . quite sure. I . . . I never even think of him."

"Why is your voice trembling, then?"

"Because . . . just because the whole experience with him was so awful. I hurt my family. Then there was Sadie. I gave up college . . . my plans for a career in photography. My whole life. I came here. I—I . . . It still upsets me to even think about him."

"How does Sadie feel about him?"

"She has her fantasies, but he's the last man I would want in her life. When you adopt her, you'll be the only father she'll ever know."

"You really think that suitcase full of iguanas meant so little?"

"I hope you aren't holding that against her. She is young, high-spirited, and I'm afraid I haven't been the best disciplinarian. But all that's going to change when you become her father. She's going to respect you and love you as soon as she gets to know you."

"She had better."

"Oh, Maurice . . . I'm so sorry we got started on Rafe and Sadie when all we should be thinking about is ourselves. We've had so little time to be alone together. You've been so patient. I've made you wait so long. You . . . don't know how important tonight is to me."

"To me, too."

"Do you believe in love? In true love?"

"I believe that the right man and the right woman can find happiness together. If other people will let them." His voice sounded a little strange.

"Other people?" she asked.

When he set her glass down, she poured him another and placed it in his hand.

"Make a toast to true love," she whispered.

"To us," he muttered.

"To true love," she said softly. "Say it."

There was only silence as he downed his glass.

When he reached for her, she suddenly lost her nerve again and shrank away.

"What's the matter, darling?"

"Maurice...I—I feel so unsure."

"Trust me," he whispered. "Trust your belief...in true love."

When she felt his hand on her breast, a shudder went through her.

"Everything is going to be all right," he said, his warm fingers sliding inside her nightgown to caress her.

The thought of Maurice's white hands on her body had always seemed alien, foreign. But tonight it was as if Rafe were stroking her, not Maurice. And his expert hands made treacherous desire flame through her.

She remembered the potion Pita had put in the champagne and the way Pita's spells had a way of backfiring. Was that why she was getting hot for Maurice by fantasizing about Rafe?

For one instant, she was tempted to go on fantasizing about Rafe and let Maurice continue. Then she was horrified at herself. It seemed so wrong, so unfair. A lie.

"I—I can't go through with it," she murmured guiltily, stumbling backward.

How was she going to go through with the wedding? She thought of her mother, of the long months of detailed planning. There were to be twelve bridesmaids and four flower girls. Her mother would never forgive her if Cathy didn't march down the aisle in that Spanish colonial chapel in her white veil and Irish-linen gown etched with handmade Venetian lace. The dress alone, a Paris original, had cost a fortune.

Armi would be apoplectic. The match had been his idea from the first. He had worried about Cathy's depression over Rafe and diligently worked to persuade her that the only way to get over Rafe was with another man. Someone suitable, of course. Armi had carefully maneuvered her into spending time with Maurice.

For a moment, Cathy just stood there, trapped, too aware of Maurice's tall, patiently waiting form. But the vision of the wedding gown that was hanging on a mannequin in her bedroom at Casa Tejas made her pulse race even more chaotically. And suddenly she knew she wasn't up to tonight.

"I'm sorry," she whispered, and then, panicking, she dashed for her bathroom, her intention to barricade herself behind the thick door until he gave up and left.

But he raced after her. As she struggled to close the door on him, he jammed his foot inside and then forced it open. She was weeping as his arm snaked out of the darkness and dragged her against his hard body. Before she could protest, his soothing hands were in her hair. His hot lips were against her mouth.

"I feel it's my duty as a Frenchman to show you how wonderful sex can be."

"No... No... I want... I want..." But she could not hurt him by speaking another man's name.

"You want me. There's nothing to be so afraid of... darling."

"No—"

But his fingers slid against her scalp, and his warm breath against her heated lips sent spiraling quivers of desire through her. Then his hands tightened, and he arched her body into his, forcing her head back, his mouth claiming hers in a bruising kiss that was so violent she could barely breathe. She fought him, pounding on his massive chest with balled fists even as his hard mouth gave her pleasure, the immensity of which she had never known.

The floor rumbled beneath their feet, and a red haze glowed around them like fire. Had Pita really wrought magic? Or was it just another baby earthquake?

Cathy's hands quit pounding and splayed weakly against his shoulders in surrender. In her imagination, it was Rafe who was kissing her, loving her.

The wanton fantasy was too powerful to resist.

So was the man.

She was supposed to be falling in love with Maurice. As usual, Pita's spell had gone a little haywire.

How many nights had she dreamed of this? Rafe had gotten into her blood. She had lain in the nights wanting the warmth of his body next to hers when she slept and in the morning when she woke, and for six and a half long years she had slept alone.

Cathy sighed, surrendering to this uncomfortable, unwanted need that made her shamelessly substitute Maurice's body for the rogue she really wanted.

Her voice dropped to a whisper. "It's been so long."

"You're hungry for this, as hungry and as starved as I am... my darling," he muttered in a mellifluous whisper that belied dark, dangerous emotion. He picked her up, and when he started toward her bed, her hands moved around his wide shoulders and clung tightly to his neck.

He released her at the foot of the bed, and they stood together for a long moment, not touching, just wanting. Then his hard mouth found hers again, his lips and tongue branding her his—forever.

One swift gesture and her nightgown and peignoir had been shredded and fell from her lush body to the floor.

Her nakedness made her shamelessly bolder, surer of her allure. She began to touch him in the way she had once touched Rafe, her fingers blind in the pitch-blackness, but skilled. One of her hands ripped his silk shirt out of his waistband. The other slipped under the silk and wandered over his lean-muscled abdomen and broad chest.

He ripped off his shirt and caught her to him. His tongue came into her mouth and mated with hers. Then his hands moved across her skin, handling her with a rough expertise that left her gasping.

He stripped off the rest of their clothes and pulled her down onto the bed, covering her with his body. His exploring fingers seemed to know every erogenous spot, and just as he knew where to touch, he knew how to touch to make her quiver and beg for more. Until soon she was melting against him.

Their passion was so fresh and wonderful that even before he entered her, in body and soul, they were one.

But when he carried her to the spiraling heights of the greatest glory she had ever known, it wasn't Maurice's name she cried out in ecstasy.

It was Rafe's.

A shudder went through them both.

Only when it was over did she realize what she had done and try to apologize.

"Maurice, I'm so sorry—" She started to roll away, feeling a desperate remorse that she had used him, but his hard hands circled her like a vise, pulling her back and pinning her tightly beneath his body.

"I feel so ashamed," she whispered brokenly. "I don't know how— Maurice, I wouldn't hurt you for the world."

"Forget it."

"It was so glorious, and I . . . I feel like I ruined everything."

"On the contrary."

She could feel him smiling tenderly in the darkness. As usual, Maurice's kindness and generous nature were the moral superior of that other rogue who would have been passionately jealous had she called out another man's name at such a moment.

"Forgive me," she whispered.

He put a gentle finger to her lips. When he spoke, his accent had never sounded quite so French. The *S* changed to a *Z*; his *R*'s rolled charmingly in that guttural way. "There *iz* nothing to forgive . . . my da-r-r-r-ling."

Then his mouth reclaimed hers, and soon they were both beyond coherent thought.

Seven

Rafe awakened groggily, with a queasy feeling in the pit of his stomach and a headache pulsing fiercely behind his hot eyelids. He was disoriented in the darkness; the only thing he knew for sure was that he had one hell of a hangover.

Then Cathy stirred beside him, and her warm fingers lightly skimming the length of his torso sent a tingle of alarm radiating through him.

He was in Mexico. There was a price on his head.

He had seduced this woman whom he loved . . . under false pretenses—again.

If she hadn't despised him before, she would now.

As the enormity of his guilt struck him, Rafe felt too sick to enjoy the blissful sensuality of her warm body cuddled against his own. Too sick to savor the immensely soothing comfort in the rightness of her legs and arms entwined around his.

She was so deliciously small, so soft and sweet-smelling. Had it not been for the guilt, he would have been profoundly happy to have her lying still and quiet beside him.

The champagne made his memories hazy. But he could remember enough to hate himself. He had believed the last thing he wanted was to be the father of the pixie-faced imp in the snapshot. But he'd found out he was, and when Cathy had admitted that she hadn't ever slept with anyone except him, a possessive joy had blazed through him. Maybe if he hadn't drunk so much champagne, his blood wouldn't have turned to fire when he'd taken her in his arms. Maybe then he would have been able to resist her even after he discovered she was fantasizing it was he making love to her instead of Maurice.

Rafe cursed himself when he remembered how she'd run from him and tried to lock herself in the bathroom. He'd grabbed her and kissed her; he had all but forced himself on her. Then—instead of confessing the truth when she'd called out *his* name and begged *his* forgiveness, he'd taken her again—the need to prove that she belonged to him in that most basic way overpowering all else.

Not that he could totally regret the sex. He liked remembering her hands tightening around the corded muscles at the base of his spine, pulling him closer and deeper inside her. He liked remembering how her thighs had encircled him, how she'd arched her body eagerly to his, begging him to love her, shuddering deeply in total surrender.

Nor could he regret the pleasure that lingered afterward when he had lain stroking her tangled hair, realizing he loved her more than ever, realizing that only in her arms had he lost his hellish loneliness.

Throughout his life, Rafe had lost too many people—his father, then his mother, and finally Cathy. After Cathy, except for Mike and Vadda, Rafe had found it increasingly difficult to form meaningful relationships. Vadda was pregnant, and when Cathy had inadvertently let him know he was Sadie's father, Rafe had thought of the photograph albums filled with pictures of Sadie. He had known he had to be part of his child's life and share that rare kind of sweetness Mike had found with Vadda.

Cathy drew in a deep breath, then let it go. The slender arm draped across his chest tensed and moved to his waist. Then she pulled her hand off him completely.

Rafe sensed the exact moment when her eyes snapped open, when she realized she was in bed with a man. He felt her stiffen and withdraw. When she sat up warily, he sat up, wary, too.

"Maurice," she said in a terse, awkward tone, primly gathering the sheets up around her neck, "I think you'd better go back to your own room before Sadie—"

"We have to talk."

"Not now. Sadie gets up very—"

Rafe leaned across Cathy's side of the bed, snapped on the light.

"Now!"

Cathy's dark eyes flashed with startled bewilderment as she leveled them on Rafe's tanned face. Before she could speak, he caught her fiercely beneath him and pinned her down.

"The brat probably inherited that early-bird trait from me, Skinny. I can't just go. I'm sure you agree this is kind of complicated."

Cathy whitened. He winced as her gaze sharpened and burned unforgivingly across his harsh features.

Then she grew so still, he thought she'd calmed down. He was conceited enough to think maybe she even liked waking up to him instead of Maurice. Smiling down at her, Rafe made the mistake of relaxing. That's when she bunched and lunged at him like an enraged cat.

But he was quicker, straddling her slim body, catching her clawing hands in one fist, and covering her mouth with his other. He found these activities to be most enjoyable—since they were both naked.

"Don't scream," he whispered as she thrashed more wildly. "I don't want to hurt you."

She sank her teeth into the fleshy part of his palm so hard, he let out a pain-filled, male yelp.

"You don't want to hurt me? That's rich! How could you be so low?" she whispered on a raw note of shame and rage. "To let me think...you were the man...I loved..."

"Maybe I am," Rafe jeered softly.

She glared up at him. "No! Not in a million years! This...this is a nightmare. I love—" She broke off mutinously.

"Say *his* name, and you're a liar!" A black fire smoldered inside Rafe. "You want to be here with *me!* You wanted to make love to *me* last night as much as I wanted to make love to you. Admit it, Cathy."

Her beautiful face was ashen. "N-no. You're wrong," she murmured in a low, choked tone.

"I'm Sadie's father and the only man you've ever slept with. You called out my name. Not his. And because of that, I'm willing to forgive and forget everything, Skinny—"

"You are not Sadie's father! Not in any sense other than...than basic biology!"

"Which is pretty damn basic." He punctuated this mild statement with a broad grin.

"You don't even know her!"

Rafe flinched. "Whose fault is that?" he growled, stung by her absurd accusation that he was somehow a negligent father. "You ran off. When I wrote, you never answered—"

"Because I knew you would lie to me again...and that I might be tempted to believe you. Do you think I wanted to have a baby alone? I—I would have told you except that..." She swallowed back the sob that rose in her throat. "Except that...I knew you wouldn't want her, except...maybe to use her existence to get more money out of Armi."

The muscles along his jaw flexed as he remembered Armi tossing the wad of bills down on top of him into that blood-spattered sewer. "You never gave me a thought," Rafe said coldly. "And as for me using Sadie to extort money from your stepfather—" Rafe's sensual mouth curved bitterly. "I wasn't for sale six and a half years ago. And I'm not for sale now. Although I'm even willing to forgive that cut, too—"

"You fool! I don't want your forgiveness! I just want you gone. Get out of here! This minute!"

"Sexual fidelity means a lot to me, Skinny," he countered softly.

"You conceited...macho...idiot! The only reason I never slept with anybody else is because the whole wretched experience with you was so distasteful, and I dreaded the thought of repeating it."

"Really? Well, you damn sure repeated it—the first chance you got to do it with me again. All I had to do was touch your hand to know how hot you were for me. You nearly jumped a foot."

"So did you!"

"I'm not denying it. And don't try to pretend you didn't enjoy the sex. Because—"

"Last night... *it* meant nothing!"

"Then why are you so upset this morning, if it meant so little?" He touched her throat, letting his fingers become a gliding caress. The instant his fingertips came in contact with her warm skin, she shivered.

Violently, she flung his hand away. "It was just the champagne," she began stiffly, primly.

"Oh—really?"

"The champagne! Pita!" A shrill new note came into Cathy's voice. Her frantic gaze flew to the empty bottle. "How... how much did we drink?"

"Every last drop. I've got a splitting headache to prove it. Why?"

Her eyes popped bigger. "Oh... oh, no reason," she said casually, and yet not casually at all. Her cheeks had gone chalky; her dark eyes blazed queerly.

"It was pretty potent stuff on an empty stomach, but I didn't make love to you because I drank too much. I made love to you because I wanted you, more than I'd ever wanted anything or anyone in my life. I feel the same way this morning, cold sober with a splitting headache, even in the middle of this ridiculous argument."

She continued to stare up at him, her pale, frozen expression growing wilder and more hysterical. "You shouldn't have pretended to be Maurice. You've ruined everything! All my plans! Pita..." Cathy opened her mouth to say more but suddenly seemed unable to choke out a single word.

"All I know is that when I took you in my arms, I couldn't help myself," Rafe said gently. "You were magic. Something came over me. The feeling was so powerful, I simply couldn't resist it. It was like a spell—''

"Stop!" she whispered in that same odd, strangled tone.

She closed her eyes. But a single tear rolled down her cheek. When he brought his hand to her cheek to wipe it away, she shrank, shivering again from his touch.

"Dear God," she moaned, her terrified eyes flying open. "It really worked. But on the wrong man! What have I done?"

"Cathy—*I love you.* Nothing else matters...except that fact...that and our beautiful daughter."

Self-consciously, Cathy averted her eyes, her color heightening. "You don't understand. What you feel isn't real."

"I know what I felt, what I'm feeling."

"No. I let Pita put something in the champagne."

Dimly, he remembered Pita in the kitchen and the pink powder and the blue flames of the stove turning green.

"Pita's mother was a famous witch. Pita concocted a potion from her mother's diary and cast a spell to make Maurice and me fall in love," Cathy said. "Only you and I...drank the champagne."

"Don't be ridiculous. Do you think I give a damn about Pita's putting something in the champagne? All that matters is that after six and a half years without you, I found you again. I love you, you little idiot, in spite of everything you did to me. And you—"

"No..." Cathy's voice was low and choked. "You really hate me, and I—I hate you. But Pita's potion makes us feel that we are attracted—"

"*We are attracted!* I don't give a damn about Pita or her dumb potion. All I know is that for years I believed you were all wrong for me. I was furious when Manuel wrote me a letter and sent me a picture of you and Sadie. But last night changed everything. I want to take you home. I want to marry you."

"Are you out of your mind?" She flashed her left hand at him. "This is reality. I'm already engaged—to Maurice. My mother has been planning this wedding for a year. Her high-society friends are already at my family's hacienda."

"So—jilt Maurice and stand up to your mother. Let her throw her rich friends a party instead of a wedding. You can't marry that titled sissy now that you've slept with me. What if you're pregnant again?"

"You're a monster. You don't understand how it is."

"Yeah—I do. Tell him you love me and that I love you."

"I would have to be crazy—"

"It's one of your more adorable traits."

"Would you quit?"

"Okay, we're both crazy." He hesitated. "The best things in life can't be planned. They just happen. Like accidents. They take us by surprise just when we think we have the whole rotten mess figured out. You either go with them. Or you lose everything. You thought you'd caught the perfect bridegroom. Instead, you're going to end up with me."

"So you really think you're going to be my... accidental bridegroom?"

"Yeah. I do." When Rafe's hand gently touched the locket nestled against her warm throat, he felt her pulse flutter beneath his fingertips. "Tell me one thing," he demanded huskily, caressing her neck. "Why are you still wearing this?"

She closed her eyes and took a deep breath. "Just go. I want my life back."

"So do I." Lightly, he kissed her head. "I never had a life...after you. You feel the same way, and it scares you."

"How could I? You lied to me. You spent time with me because you were paid to. I was just a girl—"

"You were twenty."

"I was a virgin."

"Come off it. You came on to me like a house on fire, Skinny. You wanted me the first night we met. You weren't afraid that night."

"Oh!" she lashed out, deeply upset. "You would remember only that and throw it up to me now!"

"Hey—I wasn't complaining. I was trying to set the record straight."

"You were ten years older, experienced. You knew exactly how to play me to make it look like that's how it happened. You deliberately deceived me from the first. You made yourself seem exciting to a girl who wanted to rebel against her sheltered life."

"Why were you rebelling? Because you hated that life. I bet you live in this village 'cause you still do."

"The only reason you did any of the things you did or pretended to care about me was for the money."

Rafe bristled at her cutting insults and low opinion of him. "Like a lot of rich people, you are so obsessed with your money, you let the power of it destroy everything in your life that has any real value. Okay—so you started off as a job to me. *Okay*—so Manuel promised to pay me double to keep you entertained. Okay—some of us aren't born with a silver spoon in our mouths and we have to do all sorts of disgusting things—like work—to earn a living. Back then, I had to suck up to rich people I didn't particularly like. I've handcuffed myself to all sorts of people I wished I'd never met. But I liked you. If you want to believe that the only reason I had an affair with you was because I got paid to spend time with you, go ahead. But I'll say it again. I cared about you then. And last night I found out I still do. For years, I believed *you* used me. But I want to forget the past. To start over."

"If only I could believe you ever found *me* the least little bit desirable. But Armi said—"

"Damn it! I desired you from the first moment I saw your long skinny foot and gorgeous leg coming over that wall. I didn't know who you were. I didn't care."

She sighed weakly, and he thought for a second he was gaining ground. Then Maurice's chunk of expensive ice sparked wickedly and reminded her to wonder about the plight of her fiancé. Worriedly, she glanced at Rafe. "What did you do to Maurice? Why didn't he come last night?"

"He's okay. Let's get back to the important stuff— us."

"Rafe, I asked what did you do—"

"He's okay."

She glared at him.

"He's taking a little nap in his closet."

"Why?"

"Because . . ."

"Rafe!"

"I'm afraid I handcuffed him and tied and gagged him."

"Dear God!" Forgetting she didn't have a stitch on, she threw back the sheet. Except for the loose mantle of tangled gold falling around her shoulders, her lush body was completely exposed. "I've got to let him out!"

For one long moment, Rafe stared down at her, hypnotized, the mere sight of her naked making desire flood through him. Hungrily, his eyes slid over her, lingering possessively on her full soft breasts. If he let her go to Maurice now, he would lose her forever.

"Not till I prove to you that you love me, Skinny," Rafe murmured, pulling her back into his arms.

"Never! Not in a million years. There's never been anything between us that was real. Six and a half years ago you were my paid bodyguard. You pretended to be a thief just to excite me, the way a baby-sitter would try to entertain a spoiled child with a new game. Last night, you stole Maurice's place and drank the potion that was meant for him. You shouldn't have gone to bed with me, and you don't belong here this morning. Maurice does. I don't want you. I don't even know the real you—"

"Yes, you do," Rafe said huskily. "And you will get to know me better and better. And *this* time, I promise you, there will be no more lies."

"*This* time?"

When he traced the arch of her throat with a fingertip, she shuddered slightly. "See? You're as eager for it as I am."

"N-no." When she struggled, he eased his body on top of hers, pushing her so deeply into the bed that the mattress dipped and the bedsprings groaned.

Even before he kissed her, she had begun to tremble.

Hell—so had he.

"You want me," he whispered. "Only me. The same way I want you. Only you."

"N-no." Cathy, caught off guard, uttered the negative automatically even as he began to trail his fingers over her soft curves, touching all the secret sensitive places that he knew would inflame her. "I want the keys to those handcuffs and closet. Maurice—"

"All his life he's been spoiled and pampered. It won't hurt him to cool his heels another hour or two. A rich guy like him can find another bride—easy. For me, there's only you.''

"N-no. I don't believe—''

His fingertips caressed her gently.

She shut her eyes and said weakly, "I—I thought women always chased you.''

"But you're the only one I ever wanted.''

She didn't stop him when he kissed her eyelids, her forehead, her lips... And she almost purred as he told her again and again how much he wanted her, how much he cared.

Rafe's hands moved over her, parting her legs, and neither of them even heard the soft moaning sound rising from deep within her throat when he touched her down there.

Eight

Rafe's kiss was long and thorough.

The real world seemed to drift away as Cathy felt herself sinking into a red haze of voluptuous sensuality. Only vaguely was she aware of the earth trembling beneath the bed.

Another baby earthquake?

Had Pita's spell gone haywire, or could this be love?

Cathy knew she was already lost even before her lips parted helplessly to admit his tongue. As his hands shaped her against his nakedness, her own fingers slid convulsively around his neck, guiding him down, clinging even as her fingers glided through the thick black hair at his nape.

His mouth was fused to hers, and when she felt him hot and hard and pulsating against her, she knew an exquisite happiness she had never imagined in her wildest dreams. All too soon she was returning his kisses wildly, loving the heaviness of his hot muscular body poised across her own. When he lowered his head to each breast, a fresh ripple of pleasure surged through her as his lips ate her nipples.

His long lean hands were probing, caressing, exciting her until he had her wet with desire. Then his equally talented mouth moved over her belly. Lower still, to taste the torrid essence that was hers alone. And only when she was beyond reason from his skilled, intimate tongue, only when she was beyond shame, did he drag his mouth away.

"Do you want me?" he asked softly. He did not wait for an answer, but pulled her beneath him, settling himself on top of her so that she fit him perfectly. His long legs parted hers.

When she refused to say that she did, his lips claimed hers more ruthlessly, his hands sliding over her with rough expertise. She shut her eyes, stubbornly willing herself to resist him.

"Say it," he ordered huskily against her earlobe. "Admit that you want me."

She shivered. "Why?"

"Because I don't want just your body. I want your heart and your soul."

So he could destroy her again.

"Maybe... I—I don't believe you. Armi told me about Consuelo and all those other women you *protected* and made love to."

"Damn it! I didn't touch Consuelo."

"Did you or did you not spend a week in a Peruvian jungle handcuffed to her?"

"That story has followed me for years. But it was a week fighting snakes, trying to stay alive in a flooding river on a shoddy raft after Consuelo's freedom-fighter boyfriend shot me in the shoulder. I nearly bled to death."

"Armi showed me a newspaper picture of you kissing her when a military helicopter picked you up in Bolivia. She was all over you."

"*She* was kissing *me*," Rafe drawled ominously, his voice softly arrogant. "I was too weak from the loss of blood to fight her off."

"I find that a little hard to believe."

"Look, I don't care what sordid lies your stepfather told you—you were special to me. Yes, there were other women before you. Yes, I've made a few unsatisfactory attempts since." His blue eyes shone tenderly. "But... there won't ever be any more... if you'll have me."

"How can I believe—"

"Believe this then."

Rafe's black head dipped and his mouth was suckling her breast again and Cathy felt like she was melting in a huge furnace, so great was the passionate heat that consumed her. Every part of her femininity felt swollen and moist from his kisses—achingly ready.

She wanted him so much. She would die if she couldn't have him.

Rafe withdrew and rolled away from her.

For a long moment, she lay there feeling warmly aroused, needy. He was breathing hard, too, so she was puzzled when he didn't continue. After a minute or two, she scooted nearer and pressed her hot mouth into the curve of his neck.

"Rafe..." She inhaled deeply, breathing in the scent of him, savoring it.

He shuddered. When she nibbled at his neck, his breath seemed to stop. But other than balling his fists at his side, he didn't move.

"What's wrong?" she whispered as she ran a teasing finger down his shoulder and left arm. That's when she noticed the scar where his tattoo had been. "Hey—where's your cute little Chinese dragon?"

"I stopped smoking, too. So what if I've been on a self-improvement kick," he muttered. "You're changing the subject."

"Rafe—" Gently, she kissed the scar, letting her lush breast swing against his arm, letting its fullness brush his hand.

"Say it," he ordered thickly. "Tell me you want me the way I want you. Tell me you'll make the same commitment to me that I am willing to make to you."

"But I—I'm not sure I can."

There was a fine sheen of sweat upon his forehead. His whole body felt tense and hard.

"Did you know that every night for the past six and a half years, I've gone to bed alone and lain awake—longing for you?" he rasped. "Damn it. Why can't you tell me, at least, that you thought of me...if only just once."

His words mirrored her own lonely existence without him so exactly, she wondered if he were a mind reader. "Does my saying it matter so much?"

"Yeah, it does."

"Okay," she began lightly. "So—I—I kind of missed you." But she could not conceal the tremor in her voice. "And I—I do want you. It's just that I'm afraid to trust you or my own feelings when it comes to anything deeper."

His eyes met hers. "Could you, at least, take Maurice's ring off, and promise me that you'll never put it on again?"

His gaze fixed on the huge diamond as she slid it off slowly, tugging painfully when it jammed at her knuckle. Carefully, she dropped it into a drawer in the nightstand.

But she left the drawer open and made no promises.

Rafe exhaled a long breath of satisfaction. Slowly, he pulled her on top of him, studying her for a long moment. He cupped her face in his hands and kissed the corners of each eyelid as if she were very precious to him. "You are beautiful and adorable and lovable for yourself alone," he murmured. "And someday soon, you will have enough confidence in yourself and the power of your beauty over me and in your sweetness to believe that I cared about you...and not your stepfather's money."

But he had taken the money.

"Maybe...someday," she agreed in a tight, lost voice.

Hesitantly, she ran her fingers through the thick dark hair of his chest, feeling the hard mass of muscle. With a groan, he pulled her closer against him, and, plunging inside her, lay back. She felt him encased in the sweet fluid velvet walls of her femininity, urging her to set their pace and find her own rhythm and satisfaction. And as she rocked back and forth on his massive bronzed body, with her golden hair spilling over her shoulders, with his large hands gently circling her waist, fierce waves of undulating pleasure began to course through her nerve endings, building into a dark raging storm of fiery sensation that crashed over them both, sweeping away their separate lonelinesses on that passionate tide and making them one.

When it was over, he rolled on top of her and said he had to have her again. The second time he went slower, and she felt joined to him in an ecstasy of fevered excitement. With his plundering lips and hands, with his husky endearments, he crushed her into his body and made her feel loved, cherished, completely his.

Only later did she wonder if his words and physical passion might not all be an illusion. If they might not be the results of whatever bizarre combination of herbs and natural drugs Pita had put into their champagne? Might Cathy's own astounding feelings for him be just as unreal for the same reason?

Cathy's fear of the past and uncertainty about Pita's spell mingled with her own insecurities, which stemmed from growing up feeling neglected and unloved. How could she believe in Rafe or in his love for her . . . or even in her own feelings for him, when she did not believe in herself? She reminded herself that he had come because of Sadie. Not because of her. His attitude had changed only after a lot of champagne.

If he were plagued by similar doubts, he did not show it. When he fell asleep, his black head nestled between her breasts, his hard body still pressing against hers, fresh dangers of their precarious situation assaulted her.

Rafe was a wanted man in Mexico. He had broken into her house and imprisoned Maurice. Armi would go insane if he found out. So would the Mexican police if Armi vengefully informed them. She was still engaged, and all her parents' friends were already in Mexico expecting to be guests at the grandest international wedding of the decade.

And Rafe thought the solution was as simple as she and Sadie running away with him.

Somehow, she had to free Maurice and get Rafe safely out of Mexico before Armi or the cops discovered him. Only when Rafe was safe would she be able to think about the rest. She had to find Jaime, her chauffeur, and tell him to get her car ready immediately.

Careful not to awaken Rafe, she slid out from under him and propped his head up with a pillow. She got up slowly and dressed. Removing Maurice's ring from the drawer, she studied it for a long moment before hesitantly pushing it back onto her finger.

Then she searched Rafe's clothes for the keys to the handcuffs and Maurice's closet. Her shaking fingers closed around something cold that felt like a metal pipe. She almost screamed when she realized it was the barrel of a gun. Dear God. Rafe had known very well the enormous risk he had taken to come to her.

Nervously, she dug deeper into Rafe's trouser pocket until she found the heavy skeleton key that opened her closet and the tinier key to the handcuffs. Frantically, she replaced the 9-mm automatic under the bed.

Then she tiptoed fearfully out into the dark hall, feeling only slightly easier that the house was so empty and still. Swiftly, she made her way to Sadie's room. There she found Sadie and Juanito sprawled out on the handwoven Indian carpet in the middle of the tiled floor.

Cathy smiled. Sadie always ran full-speed till she dropped. A stack of unlit beeswax candles lay spread out between the sleeping children. Cupped in the curve of Sadie's outstretched arm was the gaudy fluorescent skull, Rafe's picture and a basket half filled with wilted marigold petals.

Cathy decided not to disturb the children just yet. Closing their door, she took the keys out of her pocket and hurried to Maurice's room. But before she could touch the doorknob, the door opened.

When her thick-featured stepfather stepped out of the shadows, looming before her in the doorway like a malevolent giant, Cathy's breath slammed back into her throat. Usually, he was so loud; so different.

The fixed way Armi stared at her, the glazed intensity of his lethal black eyes, his gray face, his very silence, unnerved her. Terrified her.

Guiltily, she pushed at the tangle of fine, silky gold that fell across her face. Stumbling once more into the hall, she realized she'd forgotten to brush her hair. The minute she pulled her hand away, the unruly mass tumbled back into her eyes.

Armi looked as if he had aged ten years in the brief few days since she'd last seen him. He was gaunt, almost haggard. The circles beneath his sunken eyes were blacker than his pupils. She wondered guiltily if she had put him in this hell.

"Good morning, *hijita*." Little Daughter. "I'll take those keys," he murmured ever so softly, and yet somehow so very dangerously.

Automatically, she let the skeleton key fall into his unclenched palm. Then the smaller key. He tossed them to the uniformed officers behind him, snapping a finger toward Maurice's closet. Then he propelled Cathy by the elbow down the hall toward the stairs.

Dear God, what was he going to do? Her mind raced in terror as she thought of Rafe sleeping peacefully in her bed.

"*Papacito.*" Little Father, she whispered, "you...you don't look well."

"Neither do you. You look flushed. Like you've caught a fever. I was worried about you. We'll talk about it downstairs over coffee," he said in that soft unnerving voice that wasn't his own.

"But—"

"I must insist," he murmured tightly. His fingers bit into her arm as he led her down the stairs and through the huge kitchen door that scraped heavily across the floor. She wanted to tell him he was hurting her, but the look on his face stopped her.

Her legs were trembling with the effort of walking, her footsteps muffled and hollow because of Pita's scattered Indian rugs. In spite of the warm golden light slanting through the barred windows, the kitchen, usually her favorite room, seemed cold and implacable. Long shadows cast by these bars made a jail-like pattern across the polished, red-tiled floor. It was too early for the servants to be up, so she and Armi were alone in the vast expanse of red floors and gleaming stainless counters and copper pots.

Cathy's hand brushed a clump of red chilies hanging from the ceiling as she flipped on the lights. She felt lost in her bright earthy kitchen, trapped there with her stepfather, who suddenly seemed a dangerous stranger as he kept staring at her fixedly, coldly.

"Did Mother come, too?" Cathy asked nervously, near tears, stalling, as she poured water with unsteady hands into her coffeemaker.

"Chris was too busy preparing for your wedding. If I had told her my reasons for this visit, I would have alarmed her. Perhaps needlessly. She's worked so hard to make sure all the 'right' people come. She understands how important this wedding is to you. To Sadie. To the whole family. As I'm sure you do, *hijita.*"

"What do you mean, the whole family?" Cathy whispered as she measured the coffee grounds with a tablespoon that rattled against the kettle, wondering desperately how she could warn Rafe.

"Let us just say I would not like to make Maurice's father unhappy at such a precarious time. Just after we have negotiated a rather...delicate partnership." Armi's olive-black eyes were filled with anger as he stared at Maurice's engagement ring on her finger.

"I—I didn't realize my marriage was so important to you."

"Because you refuse to grow up. Because you chose to bury yourself alive here," he said tightly, his words soft, yet striking hard and steady like a hammer hitting an anvil. "International high finance is a risky game at best. In these troubled economic times, one false move and a man can lose everything."

"I chose to raise my daughter myself. I wanted her to grow up in an environment where she would know she was loved and wanted. Where she wouldn't have to be ashamed of not having a father."

"I should have killed that low-class bastard for what he did to you when I had the chance," Armi said, not bothering to suppress the violence he felt toward Rafe.

"No. What happened was my fault, too."

"When he took your honor, he took mine. There are only two ways for a man to pay for such a crime—marriage or death."

"That's positively medieval."

"A lot of us...down here feel that way about men who violate their women. Throughout our history, too many of our mothers and sisters and daughters have been violated. By medieval, if you mean that we haven't learned how to cover up our feelings of betrayal with a civilized veneer, perhaps you're right."

"I am an American. So is Rafe. You are supposed to be an international businessman, a cosmopolitan."

"But I was born a Mexican. When I married your mother, you became my stepdaughter, my responsibility."

"No. I am responsible for me. I *wanted* Rafe."

Armi stood up, furious. "You and I have had many battles, no?" He spoke in a weary, fed-up tone that was somehow more frightening than if he had screamed.

A potted plant crashed on the patio outside, and his attention shifted from her to the shattered pottery, spilled dirt and uprooted hibiscus blossoms on the perfectly swept terrace. She turned. Through her large barred windows, she saw that her beautiful flower gardens were crawling with uniformed *federales*.

She whirled to face her stepfather. Across the red expanse of her kitchen, their eyes met.

Hers were wide with terror.

Armi's were narrow with hatred and bitter triumph.

"I know *he* spent the night here—with you. I told him six years ago what would happen if he ever touched you again."

"He came because he just found out about Sadie," Cathy began desperately. "You have to let him go." She sank to her knees. *"I'm begging you."*

"So he can come back again and pull another stunt like this? No, I cannot let him ruin me, *hijita.*" And in a softer tone, "Or allow him to destroy your chance of happiness with Maurice."

"H-happiness..." She swallowed a sob. "I—I'll do anything you want...if only you'll let Rafe go. But if you hurt him—I swear to you that I will never, never marry Maurice or anyone else you want me to."

Armi's lips twisted. He drew a long breath. "You were a difficult child, *hijita*. You are an even more difficult woman."

"You think you own the world. You think you own my mother... and me, too."

"If you marry Maurice and make him happy... as planned, I will personally guarantee Steele's safety back to Texas. Otherwise..."

Armi hesitated, smiling as he looked past her to the *federales* and the shattered pot, smiling when he saw that she had gone pale as frightening possibilities took root in her frantic mind.

"Steele is wanted for questioning in a wreck he had with a bus yesterday. There were damages. To the bus. To a rooster."

"A rooster? You *are* mad."

"He broke into your house—he assaulted Maurice. Then there is the little matter of Hernando Guillén."

"Guillén was a murderer and a drug lord."

"Guillén has many friends in high places who want revenge against the troublesome gringo who seized him illegally and hauled him back to Texas to die. Guillén's friends are my friends. His brother is on his way to this village."

"You don't even know Rafe had anything to do with Guillén's abduction."

"I don't care, either. Why do you defend him? Surely you haven't forgotten that he extorted a small fortune from me as payment to stay away from you. He set himself up in business with my money. I bet I can persuade him into selling his rights to Sadie."

Cathy turned away, sick at heart, all her doubts about Rafe resurfacing. "He said he wants to marry me," she attempted bravely.

"Surely you don't delude yourself that he's ever been in love with you." Armi's black eyes were bright with hatred.

Before she could reply, the door scraped across the tiled floor, and an ashen Maurice walked slowly toward her. His golden hair was rumpled. He needed a shave.

Forcing a weak smile, he set a pair of handcuffs and a key on the table beside her.

Other than looking untidy and exhausted, he appeared to be fine in spite of his night in the closet. A bit guiltily, he admitted he'd spent most of the time asleep. Not that Maurice didn't proclaim rather theatrically he'd been outraged over the way Rafe had attacked him. Not that Maurice hadn't been terrified with concern for Cathy. But the closet had been so cozily dark and warm, he hadn't been able to stay awake despite his concern for her.

"Darling, are you sure you're all right?" A faint desperation lingered in Maurice's cultured voice as he pulled her unwilling body into his arms.

His touch felt alien after Rafe's. She stiffened before she grew aware of Armi's menacing presence. With an effort, she forced herself to relax.

"The scoundrel won't get away," Maurice reassured her, tracing the delicate line of her cheekbone with a perfectly manicured, soft fingertip. "He won't ever get another chance to scare either of us like that again."

Maurice's hand slid to the small of her back. He curved a finger under her chin and lifted it. Before she could protest, he silenced her with a kiss, and gathering her closer, molded her to his lean aristocratic frame.

His firm lips were not entirely unpleasant. Nor was the comforting warmth of his arms. She was truly fond of this gentle, sensitive man. But nothing about him turned her blood to fire. And she was too terrified for Rafe to be comforted.

She was still in his arms when the kitchen door scraped the floor and two *federales* with rifles kicked Rafe into the kitchen.

"Rafe," she cried out. "Dear God, what have they done—"

One of the cops jammed the butt of his rifle into the small of Rafe's spine so hard, Rafe staggered, falling forward at her feet. His wide shoulders slumped in defeat. Cathy almost cried out when she saw that there was blood in his black hair, and the cut above his eyebrow was bleeding again.

In mute horror, she sank down beside him. But when she worriedly reached out to caress his dark bruised face, he jerked savagely away from her touch. For one long minute, he regarded her icily.

The air rushed out of her body. She felt desolate. Rafe's cold look of bitter disillusionment and intense loathing made it impossible to breathe.

Slowly, Maurice lifted her limp body into his arms and crushed her to him tightly. "There's no reason for you to feel the slightest pity for this villain. Or ever be afraid of him. I promise you, this will be the last you'll ever have to see of him, my darling."

Something ugly blazed in Rafe's eyes as he looked at her. Then his dark face went blank. In spite of Rafe's obvious hatred for her, Cathy felt a strange despairing longing for him. It pulled her to him. She had a crazy wish to throw herself into his arms and beg him wildly to forgive her. But she just stood there mute and helpless with her heart hammering in her throat.

The police had beaten him so badly, his right eye was swollen shut. His nose looked bruised and lopsided.

Blood trickled from his forehead and from a deeper gash at the corner of his mouth.

She swallowed convulsively, tasting her own tears. "Rafe, I'm so sorry. I—" Since she knew what he thought, she couldn't quite meet his piercing blue gaze.

"Like hell."

"Rafe..." Her anguish pooled in her eyes.

He smiled unpleasantly. Then his face hardened until it seemed carved from the coldest stone.

"Damn you," he hissed. "I should have known better than to trust you. I should have known you'd sic your stepfather on me again. This time you won't be happy till I'm dead."

Nine

Rafe felt every painful breath squeezed through his bruised lungs and ribs where the bastards had beaten him.

What were they waiting for?

Why didn't they just kill him and get it over with?

For two godforsaken hours, Rafe had been a prisoner in Cathy's cramped living room, in this plump over-stuffed chair with the cold weight of a Colt automatic pistol nudged between his shoulder blades. He could smell the guard's unwashed body through the man's greasy and stained khaki uniform; he could smell the nauseating garlic and tequila on his breath. He knew those smells because the guard was the same creep who'd laughed when he'd strip-searched him.

Rafe hadn't looked up from the floor for an hour, but he knew he was still surrounded on all sides by the bastards. His tanned hands were folded, knotted together

limply between his knees. He was slumped forward, his
mood morose as he studied the stiff bloodstain on his
shirt and the imperfections of the rectangular saltillo tile
in front of his scuffed boots. He didn't look up, because
every time he did, all he saw was Cathy and Maurice
huddled together on the couch opposite him. And the
sight of them like that made him sick to his stomach.

Not that Cathy looked particularly happy to be re-
united with her aristocratic wimp. No—she was as pale
as porcelain and even more terrified-looking than the lily-
white Maurice. She kept twisting that ostentatious ring
she'd put back on her finger round and round. And every
time the thing flashed at him, Rafe felt tiny, vicious pin-
pricks of jealous pain. But even as he hated her, he could
tell she hadn't wanted things to go this far.

Her golden hair that was still tangled from their lovemaking encircled her angelic face like a golden halo. Rafe
couldn't look at her without remembering how soft and
passionate she'd been in his arms such a short while ago.
He couldn't bear the sight of her wanton loveliness, nor
that of Maurice's arm around her slim shoulders. Because even though she'd sold him to these devils who
would murder him the first chance they got, Rafe
couldn't entirely turn off his own unwanted proprietary
feelings toward her.

"Capitán Guillén."

The uniformed thugs' rifles shifted. Their boot heels
clicked together. The passionate show of military salutes
that swept the room were so farcelike, they disgusted
Rafe.

"*Buenos días,*" grated a smug, self-important voice.

Rafe looked up and he felt even sicker when Carlos
Guillén swaggered through the door. Guillén glared at
him with the cold glittering eyes of a viper preparing to

strike cornered prey, and Rafe knew for sure that he was going to die.

And he was afraid to die.

"*Las esposas,* the handcuffs," the captain said in that gravelly tone, chunking Rafe's handcuffs and the key onto the coffee table in front of Cathy so hard she jumped. The sight of the handcuffs so innocently resting on that cold marble burned into Rafe's brain. Guillén strutted about, studying the handcuffs and then Rafe, savoring this magnificent hour that had put an insignificant police captain on center stage.

Guillén's black eyes fixed on Rafe again as the captain took a long thin cigar out of a carved leather pouch. Guillén turned it over in his palm, the gesture oddly delicate and refined for a man whose nature was brutish. The captain lit his cigar slowly, calmly. Leaning back against the door with a self-satisfied air, the sadistic bastard ordered Pita to bring him a bottle of tequila. Pita, whose lack of love for this particular breed of macho Mexican male had kept her single for forty-two years, shuffled sulkily out of the room.

In a heavy accent Guillén said in forceful English, as if he were proud of his command of the language, "I have been looking forward to this moment, gringo, ever since you took my brother. Why you come back to Mexico?"

Cathy cried out. "No! You have the wrong man."

Just for a second, Rafe allowed himself to look at the betraying witch who had cast him into hell for the second time.

"Shut up," he snarled. "You should be happy. You got what you wanted, didn't you?"

She stared at him with those big black eyes, looking stunned and white-faced and miserably hurt.

And so damnably, so treacherously beautiful Rafe winced from the sheer pain of her golden loveliness.

"No," she whispered in a strangled tone.

"The last thing I want now is more of your lies."

The dull look of pain that flashed across her pale face made Rafe's insides clench. Her mere presence was a torment. Never in all his life had he felt so gut-wrenchingly furious at a woman or so hurt by one at the same time. He had loved her; she had borne his child. He had risked his life to come to her. He had made love to her, forgiven her and asked her to marry him. And she had gone from the warmth of his bed and handed him over to these cold-eyed killers who would finish him off as easily as a gang of vicious boys might squash a bug or pour gasoline on a cat and strike a match. He didn't delude himself he would get anything close to a fair trial. Not with Calderon paying Guillén to finish him off.

If Cathy defended him now, it was only because she lacked the stomach to face what she'd done.

Despair pressed down on him. Rafe felt terrified and alone in this corrupt enemy camp, where his civil rights could be bought from these cops by Calderon as casually and cheaply as lottery tickets from a street vendor. The danger Rafe was in was all her fault, and the knowledge of her betrayal lay as heavy as a stone in his heart.

She would pay. If he lived through this, if it was the last thing he ever did, she would pay.

"It wasn't me who took your brother, Guillén," Rafe hissed through gritted teeth. "Not that I didn't applaud the act."

"*Las esposas.* They are your trademark, no? Your friends, the Houston police, they keeled my brother. I loved heem."

"Hernando Guillén was found guilty and executed for murder."

Guillén patted his bulging shoulder holster. "As you will be, amigo."

"There is no death penalty in Mexico. What do you plan to do, shoot me in the back on the way to Mata-mores?"

"Mexico do not kill the criminals. So the family must take care of its own honor. A bullet is too easy. I have wait long time for this pleasure of playing with you the way bullfighter plays with a bull. You will die slow. *Muy despacio, mi amigo,*" Guillén said, savoring this last delicious thought in his mother tongue. He inhaled deeply from his thin cigar and blew out a long thread of smoke. An inch of ash trembled and fell to the Aubusson carpet, scorching it.

And the acrid smoke and thick smell of singed wool swirling around Rafe made him cough as if they were the stench of hell. His eyes and nose stung.

For years, Rafe had thrived on facing danger, on the challenges and risks that forced him to pit his courage and skills and strengths against terrible foes.

Mike had warned him he had a death wish, that it would catch up to him someday.

"Armi," Cathy pleaded desperately. "Help him. Do something."

"Hasn't he done enough, Cathy?" Rafe demanded cynically.

Armi threw up his hands in a gesture of mock helplessness. "Steele is in the hands of the law now—where he belongs."

"But you promised me," Cathy began.

So the witch had cut a deal. Rafe clenched his teeth so hard that a muscle ached painfully along the side of his bruised jaw where one of Guillén's thugs had clubbed him awake with a rifle butt.

Carlos Guillén smiled cruelly. "*Señorita,* your 'friend,' Señor Steele, is wanted in my country for many crimes. Yesterday, he wreck a bus and injure many peoples."

"That jalopy rammed me. I damn near died. You know damn well nobody but me was hurt."

"He molest your *novio, señorita,* an important French tourist in our country. But that is nothing compared to what he did to my brother Hernando."

Suddenly, there were childish whoops of excitement from the hall. Pita gave a little cry as the door she was waddling through while carrying a heavy tray slammed carelessly into her broad back. Pita and her tray went flying forward. Sadie and Juanito bumped into her, yelling and then they raced past her.

Guillén glanced toward the commotion at the door in annoyance just as Pita's huge tray teetered. A tequila bottle and a dozen glasses slid the length of Pita's silver tray, catching on the thick polished lip. Everyone held his breath as Pita struggled to right the tray.

There was a horrified silence as the bottle and glasses shattered onto the floor. Even the children froze for a second.

"*Lo siento, señores,*" Pita said, kneeling to pick up broken slivers of crystal from the pool of golden tequila.

"*Lo siento, Pita,*" Sadie murmured guiltily. "*Fue un accidente.*" I am sorry. It was an accident.

"Pita, leave that mess. Just get those two out of here before they do something worse," Armi snarled.

Sadie ran into her mother's protective arms and defiantly plopped her fluorescent skull down. Then she saw the handcuffs.

"Esposas," she whispered, thrilled as she picked them up along with the key. The long sleeve of her witch's costume kept falling over her wrist as she struggled to lock and unlock the handcuffs. Her pockets, bulging with beeswax candles, kept banging into the table as she worked busily.

"Put those down and leave, Sadie," Armi commanded again in Spanish.

Sadie, who had gotten the hang of the handcuffs, frowned in deep concentration as she snapped and unsnapped them.

"Sadie!" Armi yelled.

Sadie's mouth thinned. She looked up stubbornly, perhaps to assess the risk of staying where she was a minute longer, and when she did, she saw Rafe. After that, a team of wild stallions couldn't have dragged her out of the room.

Her blue eyes fastened on Rafe's face in breathless awe. "Juanito," she whispered, beckoning him to come to her.

"I told you so I saw his ghost!" he murmured, equally awestruck, hanging back.

In a trancelike state, still holding the open handcuffs, Sadie moved toward Rafe. Then, remembering her skull, she whirled dramatically, her black skirts flying, and grabbed the gaudy thing from the table. She dashed forward and placed it eagerly at Rafe's feet as if in homage.

And as the golden-haired waif looked up the length of his battered boots and filthy jeans with an expression of adoration, Rafe fell in love with her instantly despite his dire circumstances.

"Did you smell my marigolds?" she whispered softly, in the most beautiful English he had ever heard a six-year-old use, "'cause I made a path of 'em so you could find me."

"I'm not dead," he muttered softly. Then he looked up at Guillén. "Not yet, anyway. But I did come to see you."

Sadie's gaze followed Rafe's, lingering on the men with the drawn guns. "Do they want to hurt you?"

"Sadie!" Armi thundered.

"No, *Abuelito!*" Little Grandfather! "I won't let you hurt him," Sadie cried, climbing into Rafe's lap and throwing her arms around her father protectively. "Mommy, make the bad men go away."

"*Hijita!*"

Cathy inched slowly toward her daughter. "You have to go, Sadie."

"No!" the child yelled frantically, clutching her father.

When Cathy took her child's hand and tugged, the handcuffs clattered to the table. Cathy knelt down to pick them up. Quick as a flash, Sadie snatched them. In the next second, the little girl snapped one cuff around her slim mother's wrist, and in the next, Sadie locked the other around Rafe's.

Rafe jerked viciously against the steel cuff like a maddened beast, pulling Cathy against his body—hard. Caught off-balance, she grabbed his shoulders to balance herself. Her fingers dug into his flesh.

He froze when he felt her warm hands fumbling all over his body, when he caught the sweet lavender scent of her and realized he was shackled to this treacherous lying creature and had to endure the exquisite torture of her nearness.

"For God's sake, get your hands off me!" he growled.

She cringed and quickly tried to push herself away, but the handcuffs caught painfully and held their wrists together. Helplessly, she twisted at the metal vise.

As Rafe watched Cathy struggle, he saw a tear sparkle at one corner of her eye. "Darling," she whispered frantically to their daughter. "Please—you have to let us go."

"Give me the key," Rafe commanded Sadie in a hard, impatient voice.

But Sadie just giggled and backed away. "No! 'Cause Mommy might lose you again."

Before anybody could force the child to obey, the imp sprang toward the door.

Rafe pulled against the cuff again; Cathy yanked at it with equal desperation. But all they accomplished was to touch each other in ways they didn't want to and to bruise their wrists painfully again.

Rafe stared down at the handcuffs that bound his dark hand to Cathy's paler one. He felt the melting heat of her. Then his cool gaze rose slowly to Cathy's white, terrified face. He was both drawn and repelled by her fragile loveliness. The very air between them seemed charged with a thick, heavy hostility.

From the doorway, Sadie grinned. *"Me voy, Abuelito!"* I'm going, Little Grandfather! she proclaimed obediently.

"She still has the key," Cathy whispered.

"Get her!" Guillén screamed in the same instant.

Juanito chased after Sadie and slammed the door behind them. The key turned and shot the bolt.

Half a dozen officers began pounding on the locked door, but before they could force it, the floor beneath their feet trembled ever so slightly.

Then there was a crackling burst of noise outside.

High above them the mountain exploded.

The house shuddered violently.

"Dios! This is not a baby earthquake!" Pita screamed.

Village guard dogs howled in terror from their crumbling rooftops. Burros shifted and snickered wildly. Roosters crowed. Above this cacophony of terrified animal noises came the more ominous rumble of the mountain high above them as a solid cliff face broke apart.

Rafe felt the skull teeter back and forth between his ankles. He jumped up, and through the tall windows he saw massive boulders tumbling down the mountain. Huts were rupturing and collapsing across the street as the earth under them and above them broke apart.

There was a horrible smell. And he realized it was gas. Somewhere a gas line had broken.

When he tried to run, Cathy's weight held him back like a granite block.

"Move it," he yelled at her as she uttered a deep moan of terror. He yanked her up fiercely, wishing he could hate her. Instead, he felt horrible that she might get hurt. "Move it, unless you want to stay here and die."

She read the wild look in his eye and went even whiter. "Sadie," she whispered, half choking as gas filled the room. "We have to save Sadie."

"We'll save her," he said in a gentler tone.

Then the house began to undulate. Plaster rained from the ceiling as the heavy, wrought-iron chandelier above them rattled dangerously. Rafe grabbed Cathy and pulled her out from under it right before it crashed with a resounding thud onto the sofa and carpet.

The rumbling grew as loud as a hurricane tearing a forest apart or a violent surf wrecking a giant ship against a reef. The house began to shake upon its foundations. There were horrifying creakings, grindings and rasping sounds as walls and rafters broke apart, sagging inward. The odor of gas grew thicker.

Some of the Mexican officers raced out onto the balcony. Others sank to their knees and began praying passionately to the Virgin.

In the center of this storm, Guillén alone was cold-eyed and calm. With a deadly glance toward Rafe, he methodically unsnapped his holster. Just as his hand closed over his gun, Rafe lunged at him. Dragging Cathy with him, he shot his fist into Guillén's jaw. As the Mexican captain reeled backward, Cathy seized his gun. She was about to toss it away, but Rafe grabbed it from her, switched off the safety and jacked a bullet into the chamber. As Guillén got up, Rafe grinned coldly and aimed at his heart.

"Don't kill him," Cathy screamed.

Rafe glared back at her. "You would have let him murder me in cold blood."

"No... And I don't want you to be a killer—like him." Her soft face was tear-streaked; her gentle voice begged him to be merciful as she tugged at his handcuff.

Finally, he let the gun fall. Then Cathy and he were staggering toward the hall door that sagged half-open. Armi's face contorted when Rafe stopped just long enough to grab him by his thick throat and ram a fist through his jaw hard.

As Armi staggered heavily, Rafe pulled Cathy out into the hall. He was so furiously intent on escape, he hardly noticed that she hadn't resisted when he'd fought Guillén or Armi. Nor did Rafe note that he didn't have to drag her, that she came willingly, as if she were as eager to elude his pursuers as he.

When they stumbled out into the courtyard, the earth was still shuddering. The scene seemed nightmarish. People were screaming in the cobblestoned streets, and the church bells clanged in a senseless frenzy. Orange flames leaped from a broken gas line and spread to a row of low houses. There was a horrible smell of burning rubber and chemicals and living flesh.

Cathy pulled at his cuff, pointing at Sadie and Juanito, who had scaled the white wall and were climbing straight up the rocky precipice toward the mines. Guillén ran out onto the balcony. His eyes glowed like coals from hell as he raised a rifle and took careful aim at them.

Rafe yanked Cathy to the ground even before he heard the flat pop of Guillén's rifle. Cathy screamed in true terror when the bullet ricocheted inches from her face and she saw the children disappear into the abandoned mine.

The earth stopped moving when she and Rafe got to the wall. Black smoke billowed around them, screening them from Guillén so he couldn't get another clear shot as Rafe helped her over the wall. Only a few boulders were tumbling down the mountain as Rafe and Cathy clambered clumsily up over rocks, cacti and gnarled trees to the scarred face of the cliff where the ancient mine bore pierced the ridge.

They had to reach the children and get them out of the mine and somewhere to safety.

Down below, Guillén, who was not handcuffed to a woman, made it easily over the wall and climbed up rapidly after them. Right behind him were three of his men.

There was nowhere to go but higher, up the sheer rock face after the children, who had vanished into the mine.

Cacti and rocks tore their skin, their clothes. Cathy was panting and crying soundlessly from the thorns and rocks and hopelessness of it all as Rafe lifted her into the carved black hole.

The minute they were inside the mountain, the earth convulsed again.

Only a thousand times worse than before.

There was a hideous rupture high above the mine. Then a terrible rumble as if the whole mountain were flying apart. The walls of the mine vibrated noisily.

"Sadie?" Cathy screamed as everything seemed to tilt sharply.

But the children, who had gone deeper into the mine, did not answer.

Cathy began to sob in terror. Her dark eyes were blurred by her tears, her delicate features distraught and ashen.

The mountain roared louder.

"Rafe—"

Their eyes met.

Without thinking, she flung herself into his arms.

His response was just as automatic. Slowly, his arms wrapped around her, gently folding her into the hard comfort of his massive body. And as he held her, he dragged her farther inside the roughly hacked walls and away from the entrance.

Sheltered by his tall lean frame, Cathy clung to him as the walls and ceiling heaved around them. The ancient timbers above their heads groaned uneasily, sagging lower. The air outside rocked with some deafening explosion.

Rafe sank to his knees, sheltering her as he watched the avalanche through the mine entrance. Through the awful choking dust, the boulders piled up, one by one, sealing them inside the mine like mummies in a tomb.

He closed his eyes and took a deep breath as more timbers groaned over their heads. The beam above them broke in two, and falling debris slammed into his left shoulder before he could jump back. As Rafe pulled her farther into the mine, several more feet of ceiling near the entrance caved in.

He felt something warm trickle down his shoulder and realized it was his blood. He couldn't feel his left arm. His legs were so rubbery with terror he could hardly stand. With a sensation of utter horror, he watched the final rock tumble into place to close off their exit to the outside.

The last of their light went out.

The mountain was quiet.

An awful, unbearable silence coiled around them that was even more suffocating than the dust. It was cold and eternal like the deathly unbearable silence of a grave.

Rafe felt the sweat dripping from the ends of his hair. His entire body was soaked through. His fear was a palpable thing—he could taste it; he could smell it.

Cathy's arms gripped him so tightly, their bodies were as if glued together.

Terror had driven away his hate of her.

But they were buried alive.

They had not escaped.

They had come into this hellish place to die together.

Slowly. Terribly.

Just as Guillén had promised him.

And the children were missing.

Ten

Shuddering convulsively in the horrible dust that clotted her throat and lungs, Cathy opened her eyes. Thick clammy darkness lapped around her, sucking her deeper and deeper like a dangerous undertow. The mine was musty, airless—foul-smelling. And black. Blacker than hell itself.

She was sinking, drowning—claustrophobic. It was as if the black walls and ceiling of that narrow tunnel were pressing in upon her like a coffin. The minutes ticked by in that silent tomb, and if it hadn't been for Rafe's strong arms, holding her close against his warm body, she would have gone mad.

For a long moment, she just clung, her arms locked around his broad shoulders as she pressed her trembling body into the long, hard length of him. And the more she shook, the tighter he held her.

"Rafe," she whispered, choking back a weak sob. "I-I'm so scared."

She was surprised by the warm brush of his lips across her forehead. Surprised when his mouth lingered gently there for the space of a heartbeat. Surprised when his hands stroked her hair for a long moment. "So am I, Skinny," he murmured, his voice strangely soft, almost tender.

"Sadie—" A fit of coughing from the dust made Cathy double over. "Where do you think she—"

From behind her a match rasped against flint. A rosy glow blossomed instantly from around the corner. "I'm right here, Mommy," chirped Sadie. "I was waitin' for the rocks to stop."

Sadie bobbed toward them on her tiptoes, her pale pixie face golden above the single candle she held cupped in her hands. Her witch's costume was torn in places and filthy. Her ragged hem dragged behind her like a train.

Sadie's blue gaze widened as she reached up and touched the handcuffs. "I'm glad you didn't lose him again, Mommy."

"I'm glad, too," Cathy whispered, looking up as if in slow motion into Rafe's turbulent eyes.

She felt his breath catch. Then his embrace relaxed slightly as if he remembered he hated her. Still, his arms stayed around her loosely as Sadie came up and hugged them.

At the trusting love in Sadie's shining eyes as she reached up and touched his cheek, Rafe's hard face softened again. When he spoke to his child, his deep voice was tender.

Watching and listening to him, Cathy realized with a pang of profound remorse that he already loved Sadie. *Like a father.*

Numbness crept through Cathy. Suddenly, she knew what a terrible thing she had done to keep father and daughter apart. If Rafe forgave everything else, Cathy knew she couldn't blame him for hating her for that.

"Do you still have the key, *Gordita?*" Cathy asked quietly.

Sadie dug through a bulging pocket that was filled with candles. Then she rummaged through the other, finally bringing out a tightly balled fist. "Here."

Rafe took the key from his child. Since he had only his left hand free, unlocking the handcuffs was such an awkward process, Cathy tried to help him. But when her fingers touched his long lean fingers, he recoiled, pushing her hand away.

"I'll do it," he said, his voice as dry as sandpaper.

But he couldn't. No matter how hard he tried.

When he dropped the key and cursed under his breath, Sadie grabbed it eagerly and handed it to him.

But he jammed it in the lock.

Sweating now, he bent closer over their joined hands. When his damp black hair brushed Cathy's cheek, she gasped. He drew back, dropping the key again.

This time it landed on her thigh. He was about to reach for it. But his big hand froze above her leg.

At just that moment, Sadie dropped her candle, and the mine was plunged into blackness.

Panicking in the thick velvet darkness, Cathy moved too quickly and fell, toppling headlong onto Rafe's lap, her handcuffed hand wedged between the hard warmth of his legs, her mouth tantalizingly near the corner of his lips. Her other hand fluttered uncertainly against his throat.

Rafe groaned, as if in pain. "Damn it, Cathy."

Beneath her fingertips she felt his pulse beating wildly in his neck. She gulped in air when his hand moved up and cupped her breast. She could feel the burning imprint of every finger through her blouse. Something elemental hovered in the air, charging it with unwanted desire.

Her breath was bursting when he growled, "Get off me."

"I—I'm sorry. I didn't mean to fall."

Her sweet apology just made him more tense. When her handcuffed hand braced itself against his thigh so she could lever herself to get up, he swore angrily beneath his breath.

Then in the next moment, the handcuff jerked as his hands clumsily dragged her back, aligning her slim hips on top of his own thighs. Her hand groped over his thick shoulders and lean-muscled back.

His body felt hot, so hard and hot. Their breaths rasped together. He groaned in defeat, pulling her even closer. Then his angry mouth crushed hers in a bold kiss that held both bittersweet fury and desperate longing, as if he would die of the desire he felt for her.

Mouth to mouth. Hers opened, and his tongue dipped inside, tasted her, consumed her. Her breasts were pressed flat into his chest. He began kissing her everywhere, his lips on her throat, in her hair. They were both shuddering violently when a match briskly raked across the sole of a shoe. Panting hard, Rafe savagely pushed her away before Sadie could relight her candle and discover them.

Cathy was aware of his stillness, and she couldn't look at him in the golden circle of revealing light until he buried his face in his hand.

Her own heart seemed to thunder as she murmured and awkward apology. "I—I'm sorry I fell on you."

"So am I," came his terse reply.

When he looked up miserably, a pulse beating wildly in his neck, he said nothing more. She began to dig in the dirt for the key. "Why won't you at least let me help you this time?"

He nodded. "Suit yourself. I'd agree to anything—to be free of you."

She felt his eyes burning into her as she slowly inserted the key and turned it in the lock.

His handcuff snapped loose. The instant he was free, he agilely jerked his hand from hers, leaving his cuff dangling heavily as he backed away. Cathy took hers off, too, and, standing up, handed Rafe his handcuffs.

Silently, his mouth compressed, he took them, pocketing them grimly.

She felt his hatred. His suppressed fury. And all the other unwanted stuff he felt for her, too—and all of it was like a thorn in her heart.

"How many candles do you have?" Rafe asked more gently of his daughter, deliberately ignoring Cathy.

"Lots and lots of them. And Juanito has more than I do."

"Juanito! Where is he?" Cathy whispered tightly, a new fear taking hold of her.

"Looking for the way out."

"The way out—" Cathy's voice rose even though it was too soon to hope. Even though she knew the entrance was sealed and that they were buried alive.

"Juanito knows this mine real good. Ever since his mother died, he's stayed in here when he doesn't have anyplace else to go. He has food and some water, too," Sadie said. "Sugar skulls and tortillas and lots of cakes. I brought him some stuff the other day when I snuck up here to play with . . . to see if my skull really would shine in the dark.''

Before Cathy thought to remind Sadie the mine had always been strictly forbidden, Juanito's glossy black head peeped at her from around the corner.

"I found my marks," he said, his white smile big and bright in his thin face. "I think I know the way out."

Descending.
Ever deeper.

The children's candles ahead of Rafe cast an eerie mustard-colored light that lit the crevices of the roughly hacked black walls. Occasionally, Juanito would call back to them, *"Cuidado,"* careful, as he warned them to avoid some mine shaft that plunged a thousand feet into nothingness or some sharp rusting piece of abandoned mining equipment from the previous century.

Rafe had lost all sense of reality as he followed them ever deeper through those narrow winding tunnels, ducking his ebony head and hunching his wide shoulders because of the low ceilings, tramping through ankle-deep puddles of scum-filled water.

His boots were soaked through, his feet wet and raw and numb from the cold. And he still couldn't feel his left arm.

The deeper they went, the narrower the walls became. Once, when everyone else had managed to squeeze through a tight hole, he got stuck, and after thirty minutes of struggling, he told them to go on without him.

But Cathy had refused to leave him. She had coaxed him, begged him to keep trying to get through. And in that final moment when he'd felt lost and trapped and she'd pleaded so desperately, he had almost allowed himself to believe he was wrong about her. Then Maurice's ring had flashed in that sickly yellow candlelight, reminding Rafe of the bitter reality about her character, and he had lunged at her so angrily, he'd managed to get free in spite of the pain shooting through his left shoulder.

When he'd collapsed heavily onto the uneven floor, she had knelt in the muck and thrown her arms around him. He'd broken out in a cold sweat as he considered what might have happened to him if he hadn't forced himself loose. In his bruised and weakened state, the comforting warmth of her hands and her tender smile had almost softened him. Until he'd remembered her treachery. Until he'd remembered being awaken by a rifle butt slamming into his jaw. Until he'd remembered finding her in Maurice's arms. At that last memory, Rafe pushed her roughly away and staggered to his feet.

Somehow, they'd kept walking. Suddenly, they were going up, into a huge room with soaring ceilings.

Juanito gave a forlorn cry.

An avalanche had sealed the tunnel with his mark on it. A dozen tunnels went off in all directions.

Rafe felt like a rat in a maze. Which path should they pick?

Juanito chose the tunnel nearest the one he'd marked, hoping that the two linked up. But as they trudged ever farther, they found more signs of cave-ins. And no more of Juanito's marks.

Finally, Cathy was too exhausted to go on. So Rafe decided it was time they ate some of Juanito's hoarded tortillas while they rested. When they had finished eating, Rafe lay down and stretched out some distance away from Cathy and the children. To his surprise, the children left her—maybe because he was a novelty to them— and climbed into his arms, laying their heads on his chest.

And Rafe, who wanted to be hard toward Cathy, took pity on the way she looked so desolate, with her chin tucked almost into her collar, with her hands wrapped around her knees. Her golden head slumped lower. Damning himself for his weakness, he took the candle and the children and scooted closer to her.

The minute Cathy sensed his intention, she looked up, her eyes big and wet in urgent supplication. Her pale, haunted expression hypnotized him as she reached toward him, too, crawling cautiously closer, until he had no choice but to fold her into his arms as he had the children.

She sighed in shuddering relief when he cradled her close, burying her face tiredly into his shoulder. The children resettled themselves on top of both of them. Juanito yawned and closed his eyes sleepily, his thin brown hand stretching trustingly across Rafe's chest. Rafe smiled and ruffled the boy's thick black hair, remembering last night when Juanito had thought him a ghost and thrown his chicles in the air and run.

Soon everyone except Rafe had closed their eyes. And although Rafe didn't sleep until long after they did, he felt some tightness leaving him, some rightness filling him. It was as if he were no longer alone. As if the three in his arms were already his family.

Which was the most preposterous fantasy.

But despite their desperate circumstances, the fantasy warmed him through.

And finally he slept, too.

Cathy awoke alone.

To the terror and powerful stench of the murky darkness.

To the terror of knowing that Rafe had taken the children and left her.

A single candle was guttering low on the cold damp floor.

Cathy yelled Rafe's name, but the mine drowned her voice, muffled it. She sat up, and when she did, something rolled off her lap.

Candles and a box of matches.

She lit a match. Then a candle.

She screamed again and again. And every time, the tunnels swallowed her voice.

She was afraid to move for fear that maybe Rafe did intend to come back for her later.

Fool. Why would he? You kept his child from him! He thinks you betrayed him to Armi and Guillén. Rafe hates you now.

There was a sound in the distance.

She stood up, hoping it was Rafe and the children.

She screamed their names and ran toward them, but they did not answer. Suddenly, she found herself in another huge room with soaring ceilings, and the stench in the stale air had become overpowering.

A draft of the clammy air brushed her cheek. Another gust of air blew her candle out.

There was a faraway whirring noise that grew louder and louder.

Something leaped at her from out of the dark. Cold wings fluttered against her face. Something clawed the top of her head. More wings flapped against her lips, her throat.

Bats!

They flapped madly around her in the blackness, tangling in her long hair.

She was screaming and fighting, striking out at them helplessly. But there were too many.

They were all over her, suffocating her.

It was all too much. Rafe had left her to die.

She wanted to die. Slowly, her strength ebbed as the beasts hummed around her, and she sagged against the wall and slid down it, sinking deeper and deeper into the awful sickening eternal blackness of the mine.

She had fainted.

When she regained consciousness, strong hands around her waist were lifting her toward a golden light that shone high above her. Warmer air was blowing through a crack.

She thought she was dead.

In heaven or hell.

She didn't care. "No more bats," she moaned softly in terror, striking at the empty air. "Please, no more...."

Then Rafe shook her and said gently, tenderly, "They're gone. It's over. We've found the way out."

Eleven

The whirring flapped nearer in the suffocating darkness.

Rafe had left her in the cave to die—again.

Cathy drew herself up in a fetal position and lay still and rigid, cowering away from the terrible humming sound.

But they buzzed closer.

She could feel their dry wings again, fluttering nearer and nearer until they were everywhere, stirring the foul-smelling air. Their savage little fangs bit into her flesh; they were sucking her blood like furry vampires.

Dear God. She would go mad this time.

She began to scream endlessly as the winged monsters swooped and dived, hitting her face and throat, tearing into her scalp.

She screamed again and again until someone called her name from the other end of the darkened tunnel.

"Cathy?" came a deep familiar voice.

She blinked and rubbed her eyes.

Silhouetted in a gray rectangle of light was the tall lean-muscled build of a man.

"Rafe?"

He came into the bedroom and turned on the light.

He was bare-shouldered and bronzed and beautiful in spite of the tangled scars across his flat stomach and muscular rib cage, and the yellowing bruise on his left shoulder. He looked sleepy as his hand combed through his thick ebony hair, but the unruly locks defied order and tumbled across his forehead, anyway.

He was so male. So-o breathtakingly beautiful. She liked the way that black hairs grew thick at his chest, narrowing into a virile strip as they disappeared inside the waistband of his pajama bottoms.

"Rafe." The second time, she said his name in invitation.

He sank onto the bed and bent warily toward her, smoothing golden silky tangles from her sweaty forehead.

"Hey, you're safe now." His voice was kind, husky. It was the one he used with Sadie and almost never with her. "We're home."

"Home," Cathy repeated dreamily, liking the sound of that word.

Home was his ranch in the Texas hill country, on the Blanco River northeast of San Antonio.

"It's over," he whispered.

A molten warmth stole through her. His resonant voice and gentle hands in her hair made her feel boneless, almost cherished.

"Oh, Rafe, I dreamed about the bats again."

"I know. You've got a bat fixation, girl," he murmured dryly, petting her hair in that way she found so soothing. "I should never have left you there alone. But you looked so tired, and you were sleeping so soundly. We thought we saw a light. Then Juanito found the bats and remembered the way out of the mine."

Every night for a week, Cathy had had the same dream. Every night, Rafe had come to her and comforted her in this kind, almost brotherly way.

But every night, he had left her alone again when she quieted and returned to his own bed.

She did not want him as a brother.

She didn't want him to go, not tonight—not ever again. So when his arms came around her, pressing her lightly against his body, she sobbed longer than she needed to, just so he would be forced to hold her longer.

Only when she felt his lips in her hair did she lift her hands and circle his neck.

"Oh, Rafe," she murmured shudderingly into his throat. "I feel so much better when you're here."

For a magic second, she thought he wanted to be with her as much as she wanted him. But when she kissed his bristly cheek, he drew back, his handsome face harsh and flushed, as if her lips had stung him.

In his bleak blue gaze she saw everything that had happened, as well as everything that stood between them. How they had miraculously crawled out of that tiny opening three miles on the other side of the mountain. How they had hitched a ride into Mexico City in the heavily laden bed of a garbage truck. How Manuel had come to them when Rafe had called him and smuggled them across the Rio Grande in a plane that belonged to a rather unsavory "friend" who would fly anybody or anything into the United States for the right amount of cash. How the nervous, fast-talking pilot had landed on a desert road near Big Bend in west Texas, put them out in the darkness without a dime and flown back to Mexico fast—before the border patrol could catch him. How a week ago Rafe had brought her and the children to his small ranch here in the hill country. How she had called her mother from his ranch and told her what Armi had done. How her mother had told her that Pita and most of the villagers had survived the earthquake.

Not that her mother had supported Cathy's choices. "How could you do this to me?" Chris had cried. "After all the work I went to for your wedding? After all the trouble really important people went to to fly to Mexico for you?"

"Not for me, Mother. For you."

"Only a silly little fool would jilt a French count and run off with someone as awful as that—that bodyguard."

"Rafe's not awful. And he's Sadie's real father."

"He has a tattoo. And an earring."

"Not anymore. Rafe has a name, Mother."

"You've ruined us—socially, financially— You've made us the laughingstock—"

"Armi was forcing me to marry Maurice. Armi would have had Rafe killed if we hadn't run."

"I don't believe that! I know Armi was desperate to save the family...and your honor. In Mexico, a woman's reputation is all she has. If she loses it, the family loses its honor, and she can never be forgiven. She is ruined forever."

"This is not Mexico. I don't believe blackmail is honorable, either. Try to be happy for me, Mother."

"Happy? When newspapers all over the world are running dreadful stories about my daughter eloping with that awful street *thug?*"

"Rafe."

"I will hate that name till I die! All he has ever been after is your money."

"Goodbye, Mother. Maybe someday you'll understand and—"

But her mother had already hung up on her.

Rafe had shown Cathy the printed version of the story he'd fed the press—to protect Cathy and the children by telling a true account of the facts, Rafe had said. He had told a journalist in San Antonio about being hired to guard Cathy six and a half years ago, about Armi's men beating him up because he'd fallen in love with her, about having false charges brought against him in an attempt to bankrupt his fledgling security company, and more recently, about Armi setting Guillén on him in Mexico when he'd gone there to meet his daughter. Then Rafe had shown Cathy a few of the more serious stories in the financial papers that dealt with Armi's financial woes. The Dumonts were calling in several immense loans they'd made to Armi.

Rafe had told Cathy he thought it unlikely Armi would come after them now, since Armi was in Paris scrambling to convince other international bankers to believe in him, and also because too many people knew the truth.

So much had happened, so fast. Cathy closed her eyes and took a deep breath. Maybe it was too much to expect Rafe's forgiveness now, but she wanted his forgiveness so much. Warily, she opened her eyes again and looked at Rafe, who was still sitting beside her on the bed.

She hated how wary and rigid he was around her. He'd been that way all week—except the nights when her screams woke him and he came to her and comforted her. Only then did she sense that some part of him yearned for a sweeter relationship, too.

She wished with all her heart that she could convince him to forgive her. So—even though he'd already rejected her once tonight, she reached for him again, following that pulsing instinct that made her want him more than life itself.

Leaning forward, she kissed him on the lips.

"Cathy—" His body tensed from some violence storming within him. She felt the rasping brush of his fingers in her hair. Just for a moment, his mouth clung to hers, as if he found her as delicious as she found him.

She ran her fingers along his nape, winding the springy thickness of his hair over a fingertip. The scent of his skin was so earthy and clean. An all-enveloping weakness went through her limbs.

Dizzy, she swayed closer into his hard arms, her pulse thudding. But when she opened her soft lips to welcome his tongue, he drew back stiffly. She watched his face grow dark and remote.

"Cathy, don't do this," he said hoarsely, warningly.

"Please . . . just let me . . ." Her fingers curled into his shoulders. She kissed his warm throat in a frenzy of passion.

"No!" he muttered fiercely, shoving her away.

"What do you want from me?" she murmured on a strangled half sob. "You keep me here—in your house. You come to me at night when I am afraid . . ."

"I want to take this one day at a time."

The coldness in his voice flooded her with a hopeless, bottomless despair.

"All week you've been so distant. I—I feel like I am in hell."

"So do I," Rafe said, a faintly ragged edge to his breathing. "But you're the one who put us there."

"I've told you and told you that I didn't—"

He got up, his features dark with suppressed emotion. "I keep remembering rifle butts smashing into my jaw. Then I found you in the kitchen in Maurice's arms. You were wearing his ring. You still have it."

"No. I mailed it back to his family in France."

He refused to look at her.

"Rafe—"

"I'm sick of your lies. No way can you explain away what you did."

Cathy swallowed convulsively. "I just want you to love me—"

"That's not so easy."

"I can't bear that you only want Sadie, that you would give anything to eliminate me from your life."

"Is that what you think?" He gave her a derisive look. "Like I said—it's not that easy."

In the lamplight his dark face was so rawly virile and handsome, she ached with vulnerability and desire. She wondered if he had any idea how much he aroused her, how much she loved him. How could she ever make him believe she would never do anything to hurt him?

"I'm sorry. Dear God, I'm sorry," she murmured in a stricken voice. "How many times do I have to say it before you'll believe me?"

"Damn it. I don't know. You're not the only one who's miserable."

Her stomach tightened as he got up and strode silently away from her out of the bedroom, slamming the door behind him. She covered her face and sobbed quietly, listening to his thudding footsteps resounding like hollow heartbeats, growing fainter and more muffled as he strode down the hall to his own room.

He banged his own door, too. Even after that, she heard him as boards creaked from his constant pacing.

She remembered how patiently he had pretended to listen that first time when she'd tried to explain that she was innocent. And then how coldly he'd informed her he hadn't believed a single word.

He still didn't.

She knew that the only reason he even allowed her to stay with him on the ranch was because he wanted Sadie.

Dear God. What could she possibly say or do to make him change his mind and love her again?

Twelve

Rafe got up the next morning before first light and began to dress. From his window he could make out the tall brooding shapes of the cypress trees that fringed the green waters of the creek. Beyond, he saw the low, cedar-covered hills.

The air smelled cool and fresh. A whippoorwill sang. A morning dove cooed.

Usually getting home from some dangerous adventure made him happy. But he felt tired to the bone. Not that today was any different. Every morning since he'd brought Sadie and Cathy and Juanito here, he awoke more exhausted than the day before.

Going to bed without Cathy beside him when he knew he could have her put him in hell. All night he'd lain awake thinking of her warm body in that thin white nightgown, thinking of how she'd kissed him so wetly on the mouth, remembering how she'd tasted, how she'd trembled. Thinking of how hot her skin felt and how lonely and frightened and needy she seemed. As always, she'd seemed fragile and feminine and utterly lovely.

And he didn't just want her in his bed. He craved her friendship, her love. She was doing a number on him— big time. She knew all his buttons—she'd known them that first night when she'd climbed over that white wall in River Oaks, and she was still punching them. Every minute of every day.

How had he ever thought he could bring her here, keep her here, sleep in the room next to hers, and not want her? How had he ever thought he could eat at the same table, do things with her and the kids as if they were a normal couple, and stay aloof from her?

He picked up a cowboy shirt from the floor. It was the one he'd worn yesterday. It was wrinkled and maybe dirty, too, but what the hell. He put it on, anyway.

This whole family routine was driving him mad—because he knew that if he could only believe she really loved him, their life together would be heaven. But maybe he'd lived in hell too long to believe so easily in heaven. Maybe it was too damn late for heaven. Maybe he should just take her and be satisfied with what he had.

She would sleep with him. She would stay with him for a while.

Not good enough.

He wanted the whole damned fairy tale.

Or nothing at all.

He had already told Mike he was going to give up the more dangerous missions and let the younger guys do them, that he would do administrative stuff the way Mike did now. Maybe Rafe had lost his death wish. Maybe when he'd offered to give up those missions, some part of him had believed he'd have Cathy forever.

He kept waiting for his anger to leave him, for something to change.

But every time he remembered Armi and Guillén's thugs, every time he remembered she'd put Maurice's ring back on and let the wimp take her in his arms, Rafe felt abandoned all over again, and angrier and more hopeless than ever.

She had bought a cheap camera in San Antonio, and she was always taking pictures, and mostly she took pictures of him. It bothered him when he came into the living room and he found her studying those photographs as if she loved looking at them.

Every day she looked more beautiful than the day before. It was as if she went out of her way to make herself sexually attractive to him just to tempt him. They were on a ranch, but the dresses she wore were as filmy as nightgowns. Every time she moved, the soft fabric clung and swung and shivered against her knees and hips and breasts. When she stood with the light behind her, the voluptuous shape of her body was outlined. He suspected that she dressed like that on purpose, just to torture him. Her perfume got inside him and tantalized him, reminding him again of how soft and delicious she would be to taste. Every time they were in a room or a car together, she seemed to find some new opportunity to brush some part of her soft delectable body against his.

Yesterday morning, she had ridden bareback in skin-tight jeans, and when she'd acted as if she was scared to dismount, he'd gone over to help her. She'd turned her body so that she slid the length of his, so that her breasts brushed his hands, his chest.

He had felt her quiver and had flushed at the wave of desire that went through him. She had laughed and said teasingly, clinging to him, fluffing her golden hair airily with one hand, "What are you waiting for? What are you so scared of? You were scared that first night, too."

"With good reason," he'd yelled at her. Then he'd stormed off in his new truck to Mike and Vadda's.

But Cathy had won that battle, because Rafe had been so wild for her, he'd had to stay away for a whole day and night till he calmed down. But the hotter he felt for her, the colder his heart was. It was as if he was protecting himself because he didn't want to be hurt when she walked out on him again. Sooner or later, everybody had always left him.

Cathy had already walked out twice before. Both times, she'd turned him over to Armi and his goons. Both times, Rafe had nearly died, not from the physical stuff but from the emotional pain.

But knowing what she was and what she'd do the first chance she got didn't make things easier. Every time he looked at her, he still wanted her. Even when he reminded himself of what she'd done, he still hungered for her. That's why he lay awake most nights, in a cold sweat with his heart pounding, almost hating her because he loved her so much.

She'd explained that she was innocent till he was sick of hearing it.

He hadn't bothered to tell her that in his business people always lied. Even the good guys. Maybe that's why he'd become too cynical, too conditioned to believe her glib explanations that glossed over the bitter truths.

He wanted to believe her.

He would have given anything to believe her.

Which was a big part of the reason that he couldn't.

* * *

Cathy knew that things were getting worse and not better, that the harder she tried to please Rafe, the more deliberately he avoided her.

As the weeks dragged by, Rafe's coldness toward her grew so frosty she felt truly desperate. At first, he had willingly spent time with her in the company of the children. Like the day they'd gone to San Antonio and bought a new truck and then visited the zoo.

The children had been hooligans in the car lot, dashing in and out of the rows of trucks, climbing in and out of every truck bed. Rafe had been so gentle and patient with them, and yet firm, too. At the zoo, he had held Sadie high on his shoulders for an hour so she could stare hypnotically through the bars at a chosen soul mate—a lively gibbon monkey. He'd even laughed when her ice cream pop had dripped on his head, and Cathy had mopped red syrup from his forehead. Finally, Rafe had set Sadie down, and she had shown off her monkey calls, hooting until she was hoarse and exhausted and had to be carried back to the truck, where she'd slept all the way back to the ranch.

Sadie, who adored Rafe and wanted to please him, minded his softest word. Juanito was gaining weight, acting more affectionate and less independent, as if he felt maybe he was starting to belong to someone. That hunted, edgy look was leaving his big, velvet black eyes. And yet he was wary still, not quite trusting in this new country that smelled of cedar and was made of limestone. Not trusting in his new clothes and new haircut that made him stare at himself with shy pride every time he passed a mirror. Not trusting in all the new rules and new schedules. Not trusting his new fragile happiness any more than Cathy did.

Rafe had enrolled the children in the nearest consolidated elementary school, and they rode a school bus every morning. Rafe helped Sadie with her reading when she came home, while Cathy fixed supper. Rafe spent an hour every afternoon teaching Juanito English, and all through the evenings, Rafe translated everything, encouraging Juanito to repeat words dozens of times.

As if Rafe intended to keep Juanito here permanently.

She knew Rafe wanted Sadie to stay, too. But his intentions toward Cathy were less clear.

Long ago he had hired on as her bodyguard. Her mother had said all he had ever been interested in was her money. Armi had said Rafe had taken money, had started his own business with it. But although his ranch and business were still small, Cathy could tell Rafe was doing okay. His house wasn't fancy, but he had simple tastes. Other things in life seemed to be far more important to him than money.

Every day the newspapers were filled with news about the collapse of the Calderon empire. From the sound of it, Armi owed way more than he had. He had been indicted for fraud, and the once-wealthy Calderons were the last thing from rich now.

So maybe it wasn't the Calderon money that made Rafe keep her with him now.

Maybe deep down he really cared.

Hadn't he said so that morning weeks ago when he'd forced her to say she wanted him, too, before he'd made love to her?

Then Armi had come, and Guillén's men had beaten Rafe so badly there were still marks on his face and body. When he'd found her in Maurice's arms, he had believed the worst.

She wanted to believe that Rafe was just hurt because he thought she had betrayed him, that deep down, he still loved her.

For would he be so hurt if he didn't love her as desperately as she loved him?

Maybe Rafe was just scared of trusting and loving and losing again.

The same way she had always been.

She knew all about emotional insecurity. Ever since she was eight, she had been told that nobody could ever want her except for Armi's money.

Maybe she should have listened to Rafe and believed in him six and a half years ago. Maybe she should have told him about Sadie then. But she had been too spoiled and too rich and too unsure of herself to trust Rafe or to understand his needs. But that didn't mean that she hadn't grown up, that she hadn't learned from her mistakes.

Maybe he had never been after the money at all. She remembered the way he acted every night when he came to her bedroom to comfort her. At her slightest touch, his face always grew dark and flushed, and he shuddered.

He wanted her, but he was fighting himself. Torturing himself and her, too.

Now she could see they were more alike than they were different. They had been lonely, unhappy adolescents. Above all, they had both been lonely. So lonely.

She didn't want to leave him in his lonely hell any more than she wanted to live that way herself. There had to be a way to make him believe in her again.

But how?

Two mornings later, after the kids had left for school and Rafe for San Antonio, Cathy came up with the answer. She was straightening the house. As she opened a drawer in the living room to put away a couple of Juanito's pencils, she found Rafe's handcuffs and the key to them.

She picked them up and began to snap and unsnap the handcuffs as Sadie had before she'd locked them onto Rafe's and her own wrist and then scampered away—so they wouldn't lose each other again.

So they wouldn't lose each other.

Primitive childish logic.

Cathy smiled as she unlocked the handcuffs again. She was about to put them back inside the drawer. But the craziest vision formed in her mind.

With a nervous giggle, she slipped the handcuffs into her pocket and slammed the drawer.

Because now she had a plan.

The next morning, the unsuspecting Rafe finished his scrambled eggs and grits and shoved his plate aside and began correcting the last page of Juanito's math paper. Apparently, Juanito was some sort of prodigy in math. Although he was in the first grade, he was already in a sixth-grade math course.

Cathy smiled as she listened to their garbled exchange, which was conducted in a crazy combination of the worst gringo-Spanish she had ever heard and Juanito's cocky, broken English. At the toot from the highway, Old Yeller, Rafe's big Lab, ran down the driveway and barked ferociously at something on the road.

Cathy looked out the window. Through the cedar and live oaks, she saw a large yellow-and-black vehicle lumbering up the hill.

"Kids! Your bus."

"Bus," Juanito repeated, grabbing his papers, cramming them into his backpack as he put his plate into the sink.

Sadie came up to Cathy and smiled her most sparkling, impishly knowing smile. "Today?"

When Cathy nodded and kissed her, Sadie secretively opened her hand to reveal Rafe's truck keys and handcuff key shining there. Cathy hugged her tightly and then let her go.

"You won't lose him this time, Mommy."

Sadie hopped over to her father and gave him a powerful squeeze. Then the children were racing down the driveway with their heavy backpacks flopping wildly from side to side.

And the adults were left alone in the suddenly tense silence of Rafe's kitchen, which seemed way too tiny.

Cathy left the sink and poured Rafe another cup of coffee and sank onto her chair opposite him, in front of her empty plate.

The quiet of the room seemed to coil around her like a thick heaviness. With a fork, she toyed idly with a crumb of toast.

Rafe's newspaper rustled as his glossy black head and broad shoulders hunched lower behind it—as if to hide from her.

She drummed her fork on her plate.

He turned a page savagely.

The screen door creaked as Old Yeller came back and plopped himself heavily against it.

Another page flipped noisily. He wasn't reading any more than she was eating.

Never had she been more aware of Rafe than she was in his kitchen with the cool autumn breeze gusting through the half-open window above the sink. The yellow curtains she had bought in Austin were fluttering madly. The air smelled sweetly of cedar.

It would be a perfect morning to make love, if only—

She drummed her fork louder against the china.

When he closed his paper violently, her hand froze on her fork.

With a dark frown, he lifted his cup and sipped the steaming liquid. She stared at him, but his black head was lowered. And he didn't look back at her.

Coward! she wanted to scream at him. But she was just as afraid as he was.

They could have been any ordinary couple—man and wife. Having breakfast.

But they weren't.

"Why can't you even look at me?" she finally whispered.

Rafe kicked back his chair and got up. Ignoring her, he pulled an envelope from the pocket of his jacket hanging on the back of his chair, tore out a paper and threw it onto the table in front of her.

"I said why can't you look—"

"Read it," he whispered in a frozen tone.

She cleared her throat and fought back tears. As always, he was rejecting her, refusing to look at her or even speak to her about anything other than business or the children.

With shaking hands, she unfolded the crisp document and tried to read. But the black print swam before her misting eyes. She rubbed frantically at her damp lashes so he wouldn't see. "W-what does it say?"

Rafe reached for his new black hat with the green peacock feather. "It's a government paper that says Juanito stays. Mike had to pull a few strings, but it's official now."

"Oh, Rafe, that's wonderful."

This time, he did look at her before he remembered his rule not to. He took a quick breath. Then he tore his savage gaze from her face, but not in time to totally conceal the dark emotion that ravaged him.

"Yes. It's wonderful." His voice was harsh.

Her heart quickened when she realized he had picked up his jacket and was rummaging frantically for his truck keys. In another minute, he would say he was going—the way he always did, because he couldn't stand to be alone with her.

But, of course, he wasn't going anywhere. Not today. Not if she followed her plan.

Still, she was frantic to stall him.

"So what about me, Rafe?" she asked him weakly. "Do I stay, too?"

He jerked at his jacket, yanking the lining out of his pockets. "Where the hell are my keys?" he roared as she got up and came closer.

She knew just how eager he was to escape her. Her voice was quiet, dull, lost. "I—I saw Sadie playing with them."

Rafe opened a couple of kitchen drawers and slammed them shut. Then he whirled on her. "Why didn't you get them from her?"

Another little silence as Cathy edged closer. "Rafe, I asked you a question . . . about us."

"Damn it. Not now."

Softly, oh, so softly, "Then when?"

He grabbed another drawer and yanked it all the way out, rifling through it on the counter beneath the window where the light was better.

Her heart was in her throat, thudding violently, as she pulled the handcuffs out of her pocket. Not that she needed to be so careful. He wasn't looking at her.

She inhaled nervously as she locked a cuff around her wrist and then hid that hand behind her back.

He jammed the drawer into place. She sprang lightly, casually, toward him.

"I said, not now, Cathy—"

"Rafe, we have to talk. We can't put our relationship on hold forever."

He tried to push past her, but she sidestepped as agilely as a cat, cornering him.

He stiffened warily. He couldn't get past her without at least touching her—which she knew he was afraid to do.

A pause. "What do you think you're doing?" he rasped in a queer voice when she didn't budge.

"Only this—" She slid her free hand up across the broad expanse of his chest, slipping her fingers under the lapels of his shirt to toy with his collar button.

His heart pounded beneath her fingertips like thunder, but for once, he didn't jerk away.

"You like me touching you, don't you, Rafe? You like it too much." She undid the button and brushed the back of her hand gently across his throat.

"Cathy—" His voice was a low groan.

"Are you going to stay mad at me for the rest of our lives, Rafe?"

"If you're smart, you won't push me. I can't take much more."

"I know. I'm counting on it. Because I can't take much more, either."

"Where the hell are my keys?" Still, he didn't move. Her touch, her nearness, seemed to have mesmerized him.

"Sadie took them," Cathy said innocently.

"You knew she had them and you let her run off with them?" he roared.

"Bingo."

She swallowed, terror-stricken.

It was now or never.

Her heart slammed in slow, painful strokes. Then, before she could lose her nerve, quickly, like Sadie had done it, Cathy locked the other cuff around his wrist when he wasn't looking.

Cathy had wanted to get his attention.

She had it now.

He lunged back from her, dragging her with him, his blue eyes ablaze as he looked at their shackled wrists and realized what she had done.

"You little fool," he said in a low, hot voice. "Let me go."

"I can't."

He yanked his hand, and the throbbing pain that went from her shackled wrist to her elbow made her cry out.

"Why?" he whispered.

"I lie awake in the night and think of you, Rafe," she said quietly. "I've listened to you pacing. I want you to come to me. And I know you want the same thing."

"No! I don't." But his blue eyes glittered opaquely, hopelessly. Again he struggled to yank his hand free, and that twisted her soft body into his so that she felt the solid muscular length of him. When her breasts slid tightly against his chest, she felt a frisson of alarm and pleasure and exquisite desire.

He shuddered violently from her unwanted nearness. "What the hell did you go and do this for?"

"I knew you'd run off—the way you always do—if I didn't. I thought maybe we needed to spend some time together—alone."

"That's the last thing I want. I hate being around you, remembering what you did, knowing what you'll do again."

"I've said I was sorry. I said I never meant for anything to happen to you. I was so scared for you to be in Mexico that I left your bed to go get the car. Armi forced me into that kitchen. I had to go along with him and pretend I'd marry Maurice—to save you."

"Did he make you put that ring back on before you left me?"

"I did that because—"

"Don't lie to me again, damn it. You don't have to, you know." His cruel, hard voice rose. "Not when I am a man bewitched by you. Whether you're good or bad— it doesn't matter to me. You are the mother of my child. I can't get free of you even though you went back to Maurice."

"I was going to return Maurice's ring. I love you. And I want you to love me...not lust after me and despise me because you do. I don't want you to keep me just because I'm Sadie's mother."

She reached up to stroke his cheek softly, lovingly.

But he grabbed her hand, crushing her wrist in a savage grip that made her wince in pain. "If you want my love, you have an odd way of showing it." Passion blazed in his eyes as he looked down at her. "But I want you. God help me, I wish I didn't."

She had wanted his love, his tenderness. But he was feeling something entirely different, and his pent-up fury, too long denied, raged out of control. When he grabbed her, forcing her body closer to his, she screamed.

"You little fool, you shouldn't have handcuffed yourself to me." His sensual mouth curled in a nasty smile. "Because now you can't get away from me, either."

"Maybe I don't want to." But she had begun to tremble.

"You will—before I'm through. I promise you."

She shrank from the hot anger in his eyes, but he jerked her back with the handcuff, no more able to stop himself than a violent sea could stop its rage.

Then his rough hands were all over her, tearing at the pearl buttons at her neck, ripping her shirt apart. Tugging his own heavier clothes apart, too, so that his naked chest ground into her breasts as he lifted her onto the kitchen counter.

A pile of dishes crashed to the floor and shattered.

Even as she screamed again, he arched her body into his. She heard the sound of a zipper as he opened his jeans. Then his mouth covered hers in a searing kiss that took her breath away. Callused fingers glided over her breasts as he positioned himself.

Cruelly, Rafe ravaged the softness of her lips. Then his mouth moved across her throat with a fierce hunger that turned her blood to fire.

She had wanted his arms around her, his lips devouring her. She had wanted to make him realize he needed her as she needed him. But not like this. This raw and elemental passion wasn't love.

Too late she knew she should never have forced him.

Because now he was forcing her.

"I—I don't want your hatred," she whispered, her frantic voice dying even as his punishing lips possessed hers again.

"I don't hate you," he murmured raggedly a long time later, as he gripped her tighter against his mouth. "God, if only I could."

Then she was kissing him back because, even if he couldn't love her, his passion betrayed a wild, dark need that was more powerful than any force she'd ever known.

She was melting in the fire of it.

So was he.

Slowly, his rage became passion, and something else that was far more powerful.

And when it was over, she knew she had won.

The cypress leaves that had fallen from the towering trees now covered the grassy bank beside the creek like rust-colored feathers. Only they were crunchier under the blanket when Rafe rolled on top of Cathy.

They were still handcuffed together, but Sadie would be home from school in an hour with the key to release them.

Cathy was lying on her back, with her golden hair spilling everywhere, looking up through the bare gray branches at the high, thin clouds. She looked very satiated and conceitedly pleased with herself, he thought.

She had beaten him. Conquered him.

And he was glad. So glad.

Sometimes—not that he would ever admit it aloud— women were a hell of a lot smarter than men.

"It's so beautiful here," she murmured, smiling lovingly at him as she reached up and stroked his black hair.

He wondered if she thought she was going to lead him around by the nose for the rest of his life.

He certainly hoped so.

The compulsion to touch her was so overpowering, he leaned down and kissed her forehead, the tip of her nose.

"It's prettier in the summer when everything is green. The water is green and clear and cold and the air hot."

"Is that an invitation to stay here—along with Juanito?"

"It's a proposal," Rafe whispered.

"So you're not mad at me anymore?"

"I was killing myself, being mad at you like that," he admitted. "You know that."

"It took you long enough to propose. Sadie's six."

"You rejected me the first time I asked, remember?"

Her beautiful face darkened. "I hurt you, and I'm sorry. I don't want to ever do that again."

"I can't live without you," he said simply. "I don't know what I was trying to prove these last few weeks."

"We've both been stubborn. We've made mistakes. It's not so easy to trust sometimes."

He lifted their handcuffed wrists and kissed the purple bruises on her arm that were a result of so much passionate lovemaking. After the kitchen, they had made love to each other on the living room floor, in his bed and in hers. And then again when they'd taken a shower.

"You took a big risk—handcuffing yourself to me when I was so furious," he said. He admired courage more than anything.

"I had to make you face what you felt. It was a bigger risk to let the gap between us keep growing wider. Loving hurts...but not loving was hurting more. I don't care if you took money from Armi, and I didn't betray you to him in Mexico. The past is over."

Rafe drew back. "Wait a minute. I never took a dime from Armi."

"But he told me—"

"He had me beaten up, and he threw money at me in the gutter. But I left it there."

"What happened to it?"

"Frankly, I never gave much of a damn. Even later when I needed it, I was too busy trying to get over you."

"Armi said you used it to start your business."

"I borrowed the money from Vadda after she married Mike."

"I want to know more about Mike and Vadda."

"He was her bodyguard. She went for him the same way you went for me. He didn't want to marry her because he thought everybody would think he was just using her. But she's a lady who knows how to get what she wants."

"So am I."

"I know."

"And what I still want more than anything is to be your last."

"My last?"

"Your last woman, you big hunk."

"You are. You are everything—my life, my love."

"Do you know something? I never believed in magic till today. But I'm starting to now. That was some potion Pita put in our champagne."

"We didn't need Pita's potion. You cast a spell on me the first night when you climbed over that wall."

"So my big feet turned you on."

He kissed the feathery edge of her eyebrow. "Everything about you turns me on. I love you. And I always will."

"I suppose we'll have more fights."

He smiled. "Maybe we'd better keep the handcuffs around . . . just in case."

Cathy flashed a teasing look up at him. "Yes, it has been so much fun making up."

He drew her into his arms. "Something tells me the fun is just beginning."

And he knew that was true, because he knew that he would love her more with the passing of every day, just as she would love him more, too.

Epilogue

News of the wedding of one of the world's former great heiresses to her rather dashing, arrogant former bodyguard made all the newspapers.

Runaway Bride Marries Former Bodyguard blazed a London headline.

Not that the mother of the bride was delighted with the publicity. Not that the bride's stepfather gave either his blessing or the bride away. Not that anybody missed Armi, who hadn't been invited, anyway.

Cathy and Rafe's ceremony was a simple affair under a tent set up by the creek near Rafe's ranch house. Sadie was the flower girl and Juanito the beaming ring bearer. Vadda was matron of honor and Mike best man.

And as the happy couple exchanged their vows, it was obvious to all that they were deeply, madly in love.

And nobody there was prouder than the white-shawled Pita.

Because she knew that for once, that at last, she had created a spell the equal to her mother's.

The only trouble was that since she had added a dash of this and a dash of that, she was beginning to believe that she would never be able to do it again.

But maybe once was enough.

If you accidentally got it right and created a perfect magical love.

One had only to look at the tall handsome groom with his black head bent attentively to his golden bride's; one had only to note how sweetly and softly Cathy smiled back at him, to know that if ever two people had found a perfect love, Rafe and Cathy had.

Pita remembered Cathy's words, whispered to her just before the ceremony. She'd said that the greatest magic in all the world was the power of true love. Maybe, just maybe, she was right.

*   *   *   *   *

SILHOUETTE® *Desire*®

COMING NEXT MONTH

#895 AN OBSOLETE MAN—Lass Small

December's *Man of the Month,* rugged Clinton Terrell, had only sexy Wallis Witherspoon on his mind. So he trapped her on a ranch, determined to make this irresistible intellectual *his!*

#896 THE HEADSTRONG BRIDE—Joan Johnston

Children of Hawk's Way

When rancher Sam Longstreet hoodwinked curvaceous Callen Whitelaw into marrying him, he had only wanted revenge. But it didn't take long before he was falling for his headstrong bride!

#897 HOMETOWN WEDDING—Pamela Macaluso

Just Married!

Callie Harrison vowed to marry bad boy Rorke O'Neil years ago, but she bailed out before the wedding. Now Rorke was back with a secret— one Callie might not be able to forgive....

#898 MURDOCK'S FAMILY—Paula Detmer Riggs

When divorced Navy SEAL Cairn Murdock's family was threatened, he raced to their sides. Nothing, not even the burning secret he held, would prevent him from keeping the woman he'd never stopped loving safe....

#899 DARK INTENTIONS—Carole Buck

Sweet Julia Kendricks decided to help Royce Williams adjust to life in darkness after he lost his eyesight. But soon *he* was helping *her* see his true intentions....

#900 SEDUCED—Metsy Hingle

Michael Grayson didn't need love, but he *did* need a wife, in order to keep custody of his niece. So he seduced sophisticated Amanda Bennett, never expecting to fall for the fiery woman....

MILLION DOLLAR SWEEPSTAKES (III)

No purchase necessary. To enter, follow the directions published. Method of entry may vary. For eligibility, entries must be received no later than March 31, 1996. No liability is assumed for printing errors, lost, late or misdirected entries. Odds of winning are determined by the number of eligible entries distributed and received. Prizewinners will be determined no later than June 30, 1996.

Sweepstakes open to residents of the U.S. (except Puerto Rico), Canada, Europe and Taiwan who are 18 years of age or older. All applicable laws and regulations apply. Sweepstakes offer void wherever prohibited by law. Values of all prizes are in U.S. currency. This sweepstakes is presented by Torstar Corp., its subsidiaries and affiliates, in conjunction with book, merchandise and/or product offerings. For a copy of the Official Rules send a self-addressed, stamped envelope (WA residents need not affix return postage) to: MILLION DOLLAR SWEEPSTAKES (III) Rules, P.O. Box 4573, Blair, NE 68009, USA.

EXTRA BONUS PRIZE DRAWING

No purchase necessary. The Extra Bonus Prize will be awarded in a random drawing to be conducted no later than 5/30/96 from among all entries received. To qualify, entries must be received by 3/31/96 and comply with published directions. Drawing open to residents of the U.S. (except Puerto Rico), Canada, Europe and Taiwan who are 18 years of age or older. All applicable laws and regulations apply; offer void wherever prohibited by law. Odds of winning are dependent upon number of eligibile entries received. Prize is valued in U.S. currency. The offer is presented by Torstar Corp., its subsidiaries and affiliates in conjunction with book, merchandise and/or product offering. For a copy of the Official Rules governing this sweepstakes, send a self-addressed, stamped envelope (WA residents need not affix return postage) to: Extra Bonus Prize Drawing Rules, P.O. Box 4590, Blair, NE 68009, USA.

SWP-S1194

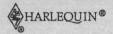 HARLEQUIN®   **V** *Silhouette*®

The movie event of the season can be the reading event of the year!

Lights... The lights go on in October when CBS presents Harlequin/Silhouette Sunday Matinee Movies. These four movies are based on bestselling Harlequin and Silhouette novels.

Camera... As the cameras roll, be the first to read the original novels the movies are based on!

Action... Through this offer, you can have these books sent directly to you! Just fill in the order form below and you could be reading the books...before the movie!

48288-4	Treacherous Beauties by Cheryl Emerson	$3.99 U.S./$4.50 CAN.	☐
83305-9	Fantasy Man by Sharon Green	$3.99 U.S./$4.50 CAN.	☐
48289-2	A Change of Place by Tracy Sinclair	$3.99 U.S./$4.50CAN.	☐
83306-7	Another Woman by Margot Dalton	$3.99 U.S./$4.50 CAN.	☐

TOTAL AMOUNT	$
POSTAGE & HANDLING	$
($1.00 for one book, 50¢ for each additional)	
APPLICABLE TAXES*	$_____
TOTAL PAYABLE	$_____
(check or money order—please do not send cash)	

To order, complete this form and send it, along with a check or money order for the total above, payable to Harlequin Books, to: **In the U.S.:** 3010 Walden Avenue, P.O. Box 9047, Buffalo, NY 14269-9047; **In Canada:** P.O. Box 613, Fort Erie, Ontario, L2A 5X3.

Name: _____

Address: _____ City: _____

State/Prov.: _____ Zip/Postal Code: _____

*New York residents remit applicable sales taxes.
Canadian residents remit applicable GST and provincial taxes.

CBSPR

"HOORAY FOR HOLLYWOOD" SWEEPSTAKES

HERE'S HOW THE SWEEPSTAKES WORKS

OFFICIAL RULES — NO PURCHASE NECESSARY

To enter, complete an Official Entry Form or hand print on a 3" x 5" card the words "HOORAY FOR HOLLYWOOD", your name and address and mail your entry in the pre-addressed envelope (if provided) or to: "Hooray for Hollywood" Sweepstakes, P.O. Box 9076, Buffalo, NY 14269-9076 or "Hooray for Hollywood" Sweepstakes, P.O. Box 637, Fort Erie, Ontario L2A 5X3. Entries must be sent via First Class Mail and be received no later than 12/31/94. No liability is assumed for lost, late or misdirected mail.

Winners will be selected in random drawings to be conducted no later than January 31, 1995 from all eligible entries received.

Grand Prize: A 7-day/6-night trip for 2 to Los Angeles, CA including round trip air transportation from commercial airport nearest winner's residence, accommodations at the Regent Beverly Wilshire Hotel, free rental car, and $1,000 spending money. (Approximate prize value which will vary dependent upon winner's residence: $5,400.00 U.S.); 500 Second Prizes: A pair of "Hollywood Star" sunglasses (prize value: $9.95 U.S. each). Winner selection is under the supervision of D.L. Blair, Inc., an independent judging organization, whose decisions are final. Grand Prize travelers must sign and return a release of liability prior to traveling. Trip must be taken by 2/1/96 and is subject to airline schedules and accommodations availability.

Sweepstakes offer is open to residents of the U.S. (except Puerto Rico) and Canada who are 18 years of age or older, except employees and immediate family members of Harlequin Enterprises, Ltd., its affiliates, subsidiaries, and all agencies, entities or persons connected with the use, marketing or conduct of this sweepstakes. All federal, state, provincial, municipal and local laws apply. Offer void wherever prohibited by law. Taxes and/or duties are the sole responsibility of the winners. Any litigation within the province of Quebec respecting the conduct and awarding of prizes may be submitted to the Regie des loteries et courses du Quebec. All prizes will be awarded; winners will be notified by mail. No substitution of prizes are permitted. Odds of winning are dependent upon the number of eligible entries received.

Potential grand prize winner must sign and return an Affidavit of Eligibility within 30 days of notification. In the event of non-compliance within this time period, prize may be awarded to an alternate winner. Prize notification returned as undeliverable may result in the awarding of prize to an alternate winner. By acceptance of their prize, winners consent to use of their names, photographs, or likenesses for purpose of advertising, trade and promotion on behalf of Harlequin Enterprises, Ltd., without further compensation unless prohibited by law. A Canadian winner must correctly answer an arithmetical skill-testing question in order to be awarded the prize.

For a list of winners (available after 2/28/95), send a separate stamped, self-addressed envelope to: Hooray for Hollywood Sweepstakes 3252 Winners, P.O. Box 4200, Blair, NE 68009.

CBSRLS

OFFICIAL ENTRY COUPON

"Hooray for Hollywood"
SWEEPSTAKES!

Yes, I'd love to win the Grand Prize — a vacation in Hollywood — or one of 500 pairs of "sunglasses of the stars"! Please enter me in the sweepstakes!

This entry must be received by December 31, 1994.
Winners will be notified by January 31, 1995.

Name _____

Address _____ Apt. _____

City _____

State/Prov. _____ Zip/Postal Code _____

Daytime phone number _____
(area code)

Mail all entries to: Hooray for Hollywood Sweepstakes,
P.O. Box 9076, Buffalo, NY 14269-9076.
In Canada, mail to: Hooray for Hollywood Sweepstakes,
P.O. Box 637, Fort Erie, ON L2A 5X3.

KCH

OFFICIAL ENTRY COUPON

"Hooray for Hollywood"
SWEEPSTAKES!

Yes, I'd love to win the Grand Prize — a vacation in Hollywood — or one of 500 pairs of "sunglasses of the stars"! Please enter me in the sweepstakes!

This entry must be received by December 31, 1994.
Winners will be notified by January 31, 1995.

Name _____

Address _____ Apt. _____

City _____

State/Prov. _____ Zip/Postal Code _____

Daytime phone number _____
(area code)

Mail all entries to: Hooray for Hollywood Sweepstakes,
P.O. Box 9076, Buffalo, NY 14269-9076.
In Canada, mail to: Hooray for Hollywood Sweepstakes,
P.O. Box 637, Fort Erie, ON L2A 5X3.

KCH